EGRET COVE

EGRET COVE

MARGARET NAVA

THORNDIKE
CHIVERS

This Large Print edition is published by Thorndike Press, Waterville, Maine, USA and by BBC Audiobooks Ltd, Bath, England.

Thorndike Press, a part of Gale, Cengage Learning.

The text of this Large Print edition is unabridged.

Other aspects of the book may vary from the original edition.

Set in 16 pt. Plantin.

Printed on permanent paper.

LIBRARY OF CONGRESS CATALOGING-IN-PUBLICATION DATA

Nava, Margaret M., 1942–
  Egret cove / by Margaret Nava.
    p. cm. — (Thorndike Press large print clean reads)
  ISBN-13: 978-1-4104-1329-1 (alk. paper)
  ISBN-10: 1-4104-1329-2 (alk. paper)
    1. Older women—Fiction. 2. Self-realization—Fiction. 3. Retirement communities—Fiction. 4. Florida—Fiction. 5. Large type books. I. Title.
  PS3614.A925E37 2009
  813'.6—dc22   2008045172

BRITISH LIBRARY CATALOGUING-IN-PUBLICATION DATA AVAILABLE

Published in 2009 in the U.S. by arrangement with BelleBooks, Inc.
Published in 2009 in the U.K. by arrangement with BelleBooks, Inc.

U.K. Hardcover: 978 1 408 43220 4 (Chivers Large Print)
U.K. Softcover: 978 1 408 43221 1 (Camden Large Print)

To all my friends in the Rio Rancho
Writers Group.
Thanks for all your encouragement and
love!

1
LETTING GO

"I've been telling you for years. You should just kiss that place goodbye and move down here."

"Yeah, right. Like moving to Florida is going to make my life any better?"

Angela Dunn had called her brother to complain about losing the job she wanted to a pimply faced teenager barely out of diapers. Instead of sympathy, all she got were smart remarks. Tony was always like that. She should have known better than to call him. But who else was there?

After thirty minutes of putting up with Tony's brotherly advice, Angela's arm was getting stiff from holding the phone so she leaned back on the bed and rested on a pillow. Getting old was such a pain.

"What's keeping you up there in Kokomo? The weather stinks, you're stuck in a dead-end job, and in case you haven't noticed, you're not getting any younger."

Tony talked as if he was an expert on his sister's life but the truth was he knew next to nothing about her. Sure, he knew she was a sixty-something community college dropout who lived alone, ate too much chocolate, and pushed sinks and toilets at a local hardware store. And if he gave it any thought at all, he might have guessed that she hadn't dated much since her husband of fifteen years cleared out their checking account and took off with a blonde yoga instructor. What he didn't know was how lonely she was, how often she cried herself to sleep, how she let people take advantage of her, or how she wondered why life had been so cruel to her. A girl just didn't discuss such things with her brother. Or anyone else for that matter.

"Listen to me, Angela. One of my neighbors is moving to Africa for a year and needs someone to housesit while he's gone. You could work for me and live in his trailer. It'd be rent-free and you wouldn't need to bring anything because the trailer is completely furnished. You could even bring that weird dog of yours. There's a dog-walking area in the park and a vet down the street. Whaddaya got to lose?"

Not much, she thought. Most of her close friends and relatives had either died or moved away and, aside from Tony and his wife who lived in an over-fifty-five trailer park in south Florida, there was no one she could turn to if she got sick or had an accident. Some of the neighbors down the street and that group at the senior center might help in a pinch but they had problems of their own and didn't have time for her. She felt like she was standing on the edge of a cliff with no one to pull her back — no one who really cared whether she lived or died. But move to Florida?

Even though she'd spent several vacations in Florida, Angela never saw herself living there. It was crowded and polluted, the summers were hot and humid, and the highways were overrun with octogenarians shuffling pristine Escalades and Studebakers back and forth from one Wal-Mart to another. Even worse, bugs the size of barn cats crawled up walls and inside cabinets, and super sized snakes and alligators lived in storm drains, dined on domestic pets, and ran amok in the Everglades. And then there were the hurricanes.

Practically begging for sympathy, Angela reminded her brother of all the sleepless nights she'd spent watching 24-hour news channels track storms that threatened the Florida coasts. With nothing but her dog and a tub of Rocky Road to protect her, she whiled away countless hours watching Geraldo-type reporters brave the wind and rain just to keep couch-bound viewers up to date on where and when the raging tempest would make landfall. Apparently misplacing the few brains God had given them, those gutsy Emmy-Award-Winning-Wannabes bent into the wind, waded through knee deep puddles, and clutched day glow rain slickers tight against their writhing bodies as they shouted out the storm's latest quadrants, wind velocity, and probability of destruction.

"When was the last time a hurricane hit my trailer?" asked Tony. He was no stranger to sarcasm and took every opportunity to use it on his sister. Angela was never quite sure if it was his way of maintaining big brother superiority or just some sort of bullheaded machismo. Either way, it always hurt.

"I know, I know you're making sense," she told her brother. "It sounds like a good deal and all but where would I live when your neighbor got back from Africa?"

Angela was looking for a way out. So far, she couldn't come up with one. All she knew was that she had no close friends, no real future, and no good reason to stay in Indiana. Life had dealt her a bad hand and it looked like the odds of things getting any better were zero to none. If the only thing she had to look forward to was growing old, she might just as well move to the land of Medicare and AARP and wait out death with all the other old fogies. At least she wouldn't be alone.

"Quit worrying," assured Tony. "We'll cross that bridge when we get there. So how about it? Wanna join the South Beach set?"

"I think the blue-haired matrons are more my speed."

"Whatever floats your boat, little sister. Just give it some thought and let me know by the end of the week. Jeff leaves in six weeks and needs to know as soon as possible."

Six weeks? Even if she wanted to, there was no way she could pick up and move that quickly. There were things she'd have to do. She'd have to sort through everything she owned, throw out a bunch of stuff, figure out how to pack the rest, talk to the landlord, call the utility companies, and close out her checking account. What for? Just to move to Florida for a year? It hardly seemed worth the effort.

For the next couple of days, Angela spent every wakeful moment trying to decide whether to take Tony up on his offer. Maybe he was right. Maybe moving to Florida would be a good thing. All she ever wanted out of life was to find someone who really cared about her. Her feelings. Her desires. But no, all she ever got was disappointment and heartache. Maybe living in Florida would change all that. Maybe it would be a whole new beginning for her. But what if she got all the way down there and found out she didn't like living in a trailer? What if she didn't like working for Tony? What if Tony's friend cut his trip short? Then where would she live? And what if her worst fears came true and a ferocious hurricane came down from heaven and swallowed up the whole state of Florida?

She spent so much time stressing over the whole thing that people at work began to notice — including the kid who took her job.

"So, what's up, Angie? You haven't been yourself lately."

Where'd he get that *Angie* bit? She hated nicknames. She really didn't want to tell the kid anything but he'd have to know sooner or later so this was as good a time as any. "I'm thinking about moving."

"Oh. Yeah. I heard some of the girls talking about it. Tired of the old pad or just looking for a bigger place?"

What a jerk. On the money she made, she could barely afford the house she was living in. Why would he ask if she was looking for something bigger?

"My brother wants me to move to Florida." She tried to make it sound as if she didn't care one way or the other.

"Wow. That's huge. But I guess lots of geezers like you move down there. Something about the sunshine and warm water being good for their old bones. Or like maybe they're just lookin' for that Fountain of Youth." He snickered at his own joke.

Angela wanted to deck the guy but he was her boss so all she said was, "Yeah, something like that." The older she got, the more difficult life became. Wasn't it supposed to get easier?

When she returned home later that day, she found a registered letter stuck into the screen door. "Super. The post office doesn't even bother getting signatures anymore." She was talking to herself again. It was something she'd been doing a lot of lately. Sometimes it bothered her; other times she just passed it off as another senior privilege.

She walked into the house, laid her purse on the kitchen table, grabbed a can of soda from the refrigerator, and sat down to read the letter. It was from her landlord.

"In accordance with recent Health Department rulings, dogs, cats, reptiles, and all other animals (excluding small birds and fish) will no longer be allowed to share occupancy of this house. Please make arrangements to immediately remove such animals or procure other living arrangements within the next sixty days."

"Is he crazy? That dog is my life. There's no way I'm getting rid of him."

Ever since her husband took off, Angela's most meaningful relationships had been with dogs she rescued from local shelters. The latest, a klutzy Aussie-mix that answered to the name of Gizmo, had one brown and one cataract-clouded blue eye. When he first came to live with Angela he banged into all the trees in the yard but after a couple of weeks he learned to avoid them and eventually got to the point he could do his business without getting into too much trouble. He had been in the yard all day but when he heard Angela's caterwauling, he barked to be let into the house.

"Can you believe this?" She waved the letter in the dog's face as he ran through the open door. "Our nitwit landlord says I have to get rid of you."

Angela always talked to her dogs. After a hard day's work, it was nice to come home and have someone to talk to — even if it was only an animal. Tony once told her that dogs couldn't really understand humans but she never bought into his skepticism. All of the dogs she'd ever owned not only understood what she was saying, sometimes they even tried to answer her. That was more than most humans did nowadays.

Gizmo stared at Angela with his good eye then curled up at her feet and went to sleep. Obviously, he wasn't too concerned about the whole situation. He seemed to know his mistress had everything under control.

"What makes him think I'd give you up just to stay put in this miserable dump? No way, buddy! I'll live in a tent first."

Angela inhaled the rest of her soda then tossed the empty can toward the trash can. After teetering on the edge for a split second, the can fell in. Next, the letter went flying across the room. A direct hit. For someone who'd never been able to sink a basket, she was showing true Olympic potential.

She grabbed the phone and called her brother.

"Looks like I'm moving to Florida."

"I knew you'd see it my way," chuckled Tony. "I even told Jeff you'd do it. Don't worry, sis, it'll end up being the smartest

15

thing you've ever done."

Angela wasn't so sure. After all, Tony had said the same thing when she got married.

Bright and early the next morning, Angela walked into the hardware store, hunted down the teenage assistant manager, and resigned her job.

"What will we do without you?" pimple face asked.

Even though she disliked the kid, she felt like she was letting him down. She'd worked in that store for fifteen years and just walking away made her feel disloyal. It also made her feel like she was destroying her only safety net. Maybe this wasn't the right thing to do after all. She hung her head and mumbled a feeble apology then ran out of the store before the boy could talk her into staying.

The next three weeks went by in a blur. There were so many things to do that Angela didn't have time to get nervous about what lay ahead. The utility companies returned her deposits, the bank offered to keep her account open in case things didn't pan out in Florida, and when he gave back her security money, the landlord asked if his letter had offended her in any way. Everything was going along smoothly. The only thing left to do was pack.

Digging through years of accumulated junk, Angela discovered outdated 8-track music cassettes, magazines with page corners folded back to indicate articles she meant to read but never got around to, several well-chewed rawhide bones, and dry cleaning tickets for clothing she had already picked up. There were pieces of mismatched, beat-up furniture, several tattered dog pillows, three sets of plastic dishes, two crock-pots, four electric coffee makers, faded curtains, and oversized sheets and blankets that didn't even fit her bed. As for clothes, there were four different sizes, none of which fit, and sweaters she never wanted to see again even if she ever had to move back to Indiana.

After packing the few things she decided to keep, she delivered some of the better discards to the senior center and then, like any self-respecting American woman, washed, tagged, and got the rest ready for a yard sale.

During the "Huge Moving Sale," Gizmo spent the day at doggy day care where he joyfully sniffed butts, slurped doggy ice cream, and tore rubber toys to ribbons while his mistress worked her fingers to the bone at home. Unlike Angela, he didn't have to stand around as neighbors and strangers quibbled over prices or complained that his treasured possessions weren't worth half what he thought they were. No sir, that privilege was reserved exclusively for his mistress who at one point got so flustered by a jeweled-belly-button teenager who called her stuff "junk" that she ended up telling the girl to take whatever she wanted for free.

Sometime around noon, Angela noticed a small girl walking around the yard. She was a pretty little thing, probably no more than six years old. She wore white silk pants, pink tennis shoes, and a long sleeved pink tee shirt with a fuzzy white teddy bear emblazoned across the front. Her red hair was done up in pigtails held in place with matching white bows and a white patent leather purse hung from one shoulder. Walking from one table to the next, she looked like a four-foot-tall fairy princess wandering through a magical kingdom of old furniture, *Melamine* cups and saucers, and costume jewelry. Angela looked around to see if a pumpkin and six white mice was parked anywhere nearby.

At one point, the girl reached into her purse and pulled out a half-eaten chocolate bar. Even though it was late October, the weather was still warm enough to melt the candy. As the girl removed part of the wrapper, some of the chocolate got on her fingers. She nonchalantly licked most of it off, but obviously not enough, because within minutes Angela started noticing brown smudges on the books and CDs laid out on one of the tables. Grabbing a handful of paper towels, she ran over to the girl who by this time had succeeded in smearing the candy on her purse.

When Angela tried to wipe the chocolate off the girl's purse, the child screamed and threw it to the ground. Two bracelets, four Dolly Parton CDs, and an antique spoon commemorating the 1963 Indiana State Fair fell out.

The little girl's mother noticed what was happening and ran to her daughter's rescue. "Take your hands off my child," she screamed.

"I wasn't touching your child," replied Angela. "I was just picking up the CDs and bracelets she took off the tables."

"How dare you call my baby a thief."

Angela hated confrontations of any kind. They made her feel lightheaded and all queasy inside. Twice in one day was too much. "I wasn't calling her a thief. All I was saying was that . . ."

The woman grabbed the child's hand and

stomped off before letting Angela finish.

When the last of the shoppers was finally gone, Angela counted the money. She was amazed. All those nickels, dimes, and quarters added up to well over six hundred dollars. She couldn't believe it. Why had she held on to that junk for so long? There were times she could have used a little extra money. For a brief moment, the idea of running yard sales for a living crossed her mind. Then she remembered the belly-button teenager and the sticky-fingered little girl and decided that working in her brother's business would be much less stressful — for everyone.

Angela boxed up all the yard sale leftovers and carted them off to the Goodwill store. Maybe someone else would get some use out of them. The good Lord knew she didn't want any of them. From here on in, she was going to simplify her life. She didn't need baggage of any kind weighing her down.

After retrieving Gizmo from the doggy day care center, she stopped off at the Colonel's for a bucket of chicken and then headed back to the empty house. Early the next morning she loaded the dog into her jam-packed SUV, slammed the tailgate shut, walked around to the front, and got into the driver's seat. Knowing there was no turning back, she took a deep breath, put the key into the ignition, and started the engine.

Then she laid her head on the steering wheel and cried.

2
NEW BEGINNINGS

Nineteen hours, five Big Mac's, two bags of tortilla chips, a twelve-pack of Mountain Dew, ten Almond Joys, one apple, and eight rest stops later, Angela pulled into the trailer park where her brother and his wife Fran lived. Tired, hot, and in desperate need of a bath, she regretted ever leaving Indiana. It had been her home for more years than she cared to think about. It was safe. It was familiar. It was where she was born and where, she once imagined, she would die.

As she pulled up to the miniature gazebo that served as a security booth, a Barney Fife look-alike obviously indoctrinated in the modus operandi of the trailer park approached her SUV. He didn't look able but he appeared ready and willing to enforce law and order or neutralize any insurrection that might erupt. Even though several drivers waiting to get into the park honked their horns, the scrawny guard took his sweet time and circled Angela's truck like a starving coyote sizing up its dinner.

"State your name and business, please." The scowl on his face and the gun at his hip defeated his feeble attempt at civility.

"I'm Angela Dunn. My brother Tony lives in this park." She had to struggle with Gizmo to keep him from jumping out the car window and attacking the guy. Then again, if the dog got out he might have done everyone in the park a huge favor.

"Pull your car to the side and try to control that dog." The tone of his voice indicated he planned on giving her the third degree. He started flagging the backed up cars and trucks past the entrance gate but one of the vehicles he let through was a black F150 belonging to Tony.

"Hey, Rambo, that's my little sister. Let her in."

Angela grinned at her brother and silently mouthed the word "Rambo?" Tony just laughed and motioned for her to follow. Waving cheerfully, she breezed through the gate and past the befuddled guard.

Although she'd been to the park several times, Angela had never really looked around. Now, as if for the first time, she noticed the wide streets, the skillfully pruned trees and shrubs, and the freshly clipped grass. What impressed her most, however, was not what she saw — it was what she didn't see. There were no trailers more than ten years old, no junky cars, no peeling paint, no cracked driveways, and no Big Wheels. There wasn't a garbage can, empty or full, anywhere in sight, and there were no stray dogs, cats, or overgrown iguanas running loose and terrorizing the neighborhood's avian population. The place oozed class.

Tony drove past his trailer, a doublewide with bonsai boxwoods and a five-foot-tall Grecian statue in the yard, and parked in front of a small but homey looking single-wide three doors down. The yellow shutters on the windows, tropical-looking green plants hanging from the eaves, and the screened sunroom made it look like something from *Gone with the Wind.* The only thing missing were white columns. Definitely something she would add if she decided to stay.

"I wasn't expecting you until tomorrow. What'd you do, drive straight through?" Tony propelled his portly six-foot frame out of his truck, yanked open Angela's door, and dragged her out before she could caution him about Gizmo.

"Quick. Grab the dog. He's half blind and

might get away."

Gizmo was balancing on three legs, aiming at a short birdbath. Lucky for the birds, he missed.

"Looks like he just needed a potty break. Come on, boy, your mother is worried you'll get in trouble."

As Tony grabbed the dog by the collar and led him back to the car, Angela noticed her brother's once-raven hair was thinning and white. It also looked like he'd put on about twenty five pounds since she'd last seen him. How long ago had that been? Two years? Three years? She couldn't remember.

After giving his sister a bear hug, Tony turned toward the small trailer. "Well, this is it," he announced. "Whaddaya think?"

"You're kidding. This is your friend's trailer?"

"We don't call them trailers down here. We call them manufactured homes." Tony pretended to be offended.

"Excuuuuz me. Hope no one was listening."

"Just in case, let's get you inside before Rambo sends the lynch mob out."

When Tony first told Angela about the trailer, she envisioned small rooms, mildew stained woodwork, and discount store furniture. Much to her surprise, she walked into a living room furnished with white wicker settees, pastel cushions, and expensive looking watercolors that depicted the Florida of a forgotten time. In the kitchen there were almond-colored appliances, a bay-windowed breakfast nook, and pinkish oak kitchen cabinets. Off to one side, a short hall led to the only bedroom. The room took up the width of the trailer and was decorated in restful shades of peach and lime green. Just beyond the bedroom, there was a bathroom complete with an octagonal garden tub surrounded with green plants, scented candles, and a crystal bowl filled with hotel sized soaps, bath crystals, shampoos, and body lotions. Everything was so luxurious that Angela had a hard time believing the trailer belonged to a man.

"What'd you say this guy does for a living?"

"He's a doctor. Used to be some big mucky-muck surgeon out in California but he gave it all up and moved down here a few years ago. Now he travels around the world and works for Doctors Without Borders. That's why he's in Africa."

"Maybe he should have taken up interior decorating. This place is gorgeous."

"Actually, I think it was like this when he bought it. He's only been here a couple of years but he travels around so much he probably hasn't had time to change anything. Like it?"

"*Like* isn't the word. It's nicer than any hotel I've ever stayed in." She was walking around, picking things up, and looking at labels. Someone sure had expensive taste.

"Don't get out much, do ya?"

Angela playfully pushed her brother toward the door. "I think I hear Fran calling you. Why don't you just go home and let me and the dog get settled?"

"Guess I know where I'm not wanted." Tony was laughing as he walked toward his truck.

Still marveling at her good fortune, Angela decided to give herself a well-deserved dip in the alluring tub. Her grandmother always said that bathing was the supreme gift of the spiritual civilization. Even at a young age, she took that to mean that a good soak soothed the body as well as the soul. That was just what she needed.

While the water was running, she poured in some bath crystals. A delicate fragrance filled the room. "Now, don't tell me those bath crystals were left over by some former owner. Maybe the good doctor must have a lady friend. What do you think, boy?"

Gizmo laid spread eagled on the tile floor

27

outside the open bathroom door. Even though it was ninety degrees outside, the trailer was deliciously cool and he was taking full advantage of finally being free of the car.

"Remind me to thank Tony for turning the air conditioning on."

The dog's only response was a muffled yip and a few leg jerks. He was having puppy dreams.

Angela slid into the tub and laid her head against the small pillow that hung across the back. The warm water and gentle bubbles felt pleasant against her skin. She closed her eyes and took a deep breath. When she started to yawn, she realized how tired she was. "Better not get too comfortable. If I fall asleep in this tub, I'll probably drown. Then Tony will have to come over and pull me out. Yikes!"

Finishing her bath, she wrapped herself in a fluffy peach colored towel then put on fresh clothes. After the long road trip, it felt invigorating to be clean and she promised herself that if she ever had to travel that far again, she'd definitely fly.

Heading for the kitchen, she called out to Gizmo. "Are you hungry, boy?"

Rising from his well-deserved nap, the dog extended his front legs, tipped his head back, and stretched his dreams away. Angela couldn't tell who was more tired — her or the dog.

As she finished dishing out the dog food and laid the bowl on the floor, she heard a knock at the door. Abandoning his dinner, Gizmo ran to see who it was.

"Cool it, boy. It's probably just Tony."

When she opened the door Angela was surprised to find a svelte-looking gentleman wearing an azure blue shirt (open to the third button) and white trousers that had sharp creases but no wrinkles. Polyester in Florida? No way.

"*Ciao.* My name is Gilberto Fontero, and I would like to welcome you to Egret Cove."

Angela immediately recognized her unexpected caller as the man Tony once described as an aging lothario who came on to all the women in the park. At first she wasn't sure if it was smart to let him in but when he tempted her with an overflowing platter of antipasto and a chilled bottle of wine she decided it was worth a chance and quickly led him to the sunroom.

"Is this your first trip to Florida?" He removed the cork from the wine and poured a small amount into Angela's glass.

"No, I've been here a bunch of times." She held the glass to her nose, slowly

29

swirled the liquid, breathed in its delicate fragrance, and then sampled the white nectar.

"Umm. That's nice."

"Yes. It is a Pinot Grigio. From Italy, of course." He filled her glass and poured some for himself.

"So how is it we have never met?"

"I usually came out during the holidays to visit my brother and his wife but there was always so much going on that I never had a chance to meet any of their neighbors. Maybe things will be different now that I'll be staying around for a while."

The bath must have stimulated her appetite because, all of a sudden, Angela was famished. She popped a calamato olive into her mouth and followed it with a piece of provolone cheese.

"I know Tony and Fran well." Gilberto leaned back in his chair and gazed directly into Angela's eyes. "They are good people. Tony says you will be working for him. Do you know anything about his business?"

"Not much. Just that he's an exterminator. From what I hear, that's a pretty good business around here. I'm not sure I'm gonna like it but, like they say, it's a living."

"What did you do in Indiana?" He attempted to pour more wine for Angela but she put a hand over her glass and shook her head. Aside from the fact that she wasn't much of a drinker, she didn't want to give her new neighbor the wrong impression.

"I worked for one of those big box hardware stores. I got to know a lot about paint, and plumbing, and stuff and I really enjoyed it at first. But after giving them fifteen years of my life they gave the job I wanted to a kid barely out of diapers." She chomped down on a chunk of salami.

"That must have really upset you."

"Yes. But to make matters even worse, my landlord sent me a letter saying I had to get rid of my dog. So when Tony told me about this house-sitting job I figured I didn't have anything to lose."

"It must have been very difficult for you to pick up and leave everything behind."

"Well, it had its ups and downs. Giving up my job was no great tragedy. In fact, I learned enough to know I'll never work in retail again. Driving down here was the real problem. It rained all the way, my arthritis bothered me, and since I'm divorced and didn't have any friends that could come with me, I was all alone except for my dog. I had a can of pepper spray in the car but I was too afraid to stay alone in a motel so I drove straight through." She realized she

31

was giving the curious stranger way too much information and quickly changed the subject. "But enough about me. What brought you to Florida?"

"Oh, that is a long and boring story. I am sure you do not want to hear it."

"Yes, I do." Anything was better than talking about Indiana. It seemed like a lifetime ago and she didn't want to open the door to the past. The sob stories could wait for another time — if there ever was one.

"Well, my family and I came to the United States from Italy in 1925. I was just a baby but somehow I remember the way Ellis Island looked and smelled as we came through. There were so many people pushing and shoving. Some were Poles, some were Russians, but the Italians stood out because they all carried their own garlic, cheese, and red wine." He leaned forward in his chair and forked a peperoncini.

"I was baptized Francisco before we left Italy but on the boat trip over my mother started calling me Gilberto, which means *My Joy,* and the name stuck. You see, I was her only son so I was special to her.

"We lived in New York for a while but the cold, wet winters were hard on Mother. My father packed us all up, I had four sisters by then, and moved us to Florida. Those were tough times but my father opened a small restaurant and served food like in the old country. People came from all over the state just to eat his food. They said it was like going home." He spoke with so much passion that Angela found herself becoming engrossed in his story.

"The restaurant suffered during the Great Depression so my mother went to work in the orange groves but her health was bad and we lost her in 1937. Two years later the New Yorker Hotel opened in Miami and I took a part-time job there as a bellboy. It was around that same time that my father decided to leave us."

"You mean . . ."

"Yes. He just quit eating. He could not stand being away from my mother, so he went to be with her."

"I think I'll take a little bit more of that wine now." For some reason, the wine seemed especially comforting.

"Anyway, knowing I had to take care of my sisters, I quit school and went to work full time. I started out as a waiter, worked my way up to maitre d', and then decided to follow in my father's footsteps. I moved into the kitchen, worked with some great chefs, learned everything I could, and eventually became the head chef at the hotel's restaurant. That job put all four of my sisters through college. Two of them got married and gave me lots of nieces and nephews, one became a nun, and one was frail like my mother and left us at an early age."

"Wow. Do you still work at the hotel?"

"Unfortunately, no. It was demolished in 1981. I hated to see it go because it had been a big part of my life for more than forty years. But the hotel gave me such a generous pension that I was able to retire and move here."

"Did you ever marry?"

"Yes. Twice. But both of my wives left me and now, I am alone."

"That's sad." Angela finished off the cheese and salami and started working on the marinated mushrooms and artichoke hearts.

"Not really. Being married had its good points but being single was better because it gave me freedom and allowed me to do the things I wanted to do. I traveled a lot, ate a lot of delicious food, and drank a lot of good wine. I got to see all Seven Wonders of the Ancient World, and I learned several different languages. It was good to get out and be on my own but I always enjoyed getting back to the hotel because of all the interest-

34

ing people I met there."

"Anyone famous?"

"Oh yes. I met Liberace, Jackie Gleason, Sid Caesar and Imogene Coca, Frank Sinatra and his mob, and that great Italian lover, Rossano Brazzi."

"You mean the guy from *South Pacific*?"

"Yes. Whenever he was in town, he came to the restaurant and ordered my osso bucco. He said it was the best he had ever tasted."

What's osso . . . ?" Angela thought she knew all about Italian food. Was her worldly neighbor trying to pull a fast one on her?

"Osso bucco? I guess you could call it veal stew. There are many different recipes but I make mine with carrots, onions, white wine, plenty of garlic, and just a hint of rosemary."

"Sounds yummy." She finished off the last of the mushrooms and licked her fingers.

"I would be honored to make it for you sometime. Maybe next weekend?"

Tony was right about the flirtatious Italian. He hardly knew her and he was already offering to cook for her. Smooth move but he could have waited until she got a little more settled in. She was going to have to be careful around this guy.

Just as Gilberto suggested another bottle of wine, the telephone rang. It was Fran saying she'd stocked the refrigerator with enough food to last a lifetime and asking if Angela would like to join them for dinner on Saturday night. "We're going to grill some steaks and have a few neighbors over. It would be a good time for you to meet them."

"I've already met one," replied Angela.

"Don't tell me," snickered Fran. "It's Gilberto, isn't it?"

"How'd you guess?"

"I know my neighbors."

"So what do people wear to Florida cookouts?" Angela thought about the clothes packed away in her suitcases. Mostly jeans and tee shirts, she wondered if she had anything suitable.

"Something comfortable," replied Fran "Like maybe a sundress or a cute shorts outfit."

"I don't think I have anything like that."

"Sounds like someone needs to go shopping."

3
PARTY TIME

Feeling like a cheap retread going flat, Angela dragged herself out of bed, splashed cold water on her face, and got dressed. Even though she was worn out after her long road trip, there was no way around it. If she was going to meet her brother's friends she'd have to go shopping. Cut-offs and tee shirts might be acceptable in Indiana but they probably wouldn't pass muster in Florida.

Almost immediately, she knew she'd made a mistake. Trying to get on a Florida freeway on a Saturday morning had to be as foolhardy as driving the wrong way on the Indianapolis Speedway during the Memorial Day 500. All those drivers who steered clear of rush hour traffic during the week made a mad dash for the roads on the weekends. She tried to go with the flow but there were so many people darting in and out in front of her she began to think they were doing it on purpose.

Had they spotted her Indiana license plates? Daredevils whipped by at breakneck speeds, oblivious geriatrics crept along in the passing lane, and hardly anyone used that lever on the left side of the steering column. Either they didn't know it was there or they'd forgotten it was there. Even worse, somewhere along the way all the highway exit numbers had been changed and now the off ramp signboards displayed both the old and new numbers. Locals might have known where they were going but Angela was clueless so she picked the closest exit, pulled off the highway, and then whispered a silent prayer of thanks that neither she nor her vehicle had been wiped off the face of the earth.

Just beyond the exit, she spotted the mall. "Hey, lookee there. Not bad for a hick from the sticks."

Looking more like a tropical resort than a shopping center, the mall was a mind-boggling array of palm trees, water fountains, glitzy specialty shops, restaurants, movie theaters, video arcades, and sports bars. It was the kind of place where women could shop for the latest fashions while their kids waged war against cyber-villains and their husbands kibitzed with friends or kept tabs on their beloved home teams.

Angela quickly located the store Fran recommended and was beginning to look through the walking shorts when a buxom sales woman strutted across the room. Instead of just asking if she could help (a question that could be answered with a curt "NO") the over-zealous woman launched into telling Angela all about the "fabulous" sale the store was having and how she should check out the sundresses.

The woman's hair was fire-engine red but judging from the spots on her hands and the wrinkles on her neck it was obvious that the color came from a bottle. "We've got an emerald green number that would be just perfect for you. It's as pretty as a picture and it will set off your beautiful gray hair." Grabbing an armful of dresses, she led a reluctant Angela to the fitting rooms.

For the next two hours, Angela tried on at least fifteen different dresses but ended up choosing the green one. "Old Red was right," she thought. "This dress even makes me look younger. Now if I could just do something about the bags under my eyes, we'd be in business."

When Angela finally handed the sales woman her credit card, she thanked her for her help. "You sure know your stuff."

"I like to keep my customers happy. Next time you need anything, come see me. My name is Katherine Burns and I'm the department manager here."

"Great, Katherine. I'll remember that."

Angela was so pleased with the dress that she stopped at a beauty shop, got her long, gray ponytail swept up off the back of her neck, and then visited a couple more stores where she bought trendy sandals and chandelier earrings to complete her "young look." She'd spent most of what was left of the yard sale money but it was worth it. If all went right, she'd knock 'em dead at Tony's party.

By the time she made her way to the parking lot, it was almost four o'clock. Instead of jumping back on the freeway she chose a surface route that was more congested but less nerve-racking. An hour later she pulled into the trailer park, waved a haughty hello to Rambo, and drove on to Jeff's trailer.

With only an hour to spare, she hurriedly fed and walked Gizmo, took a quick shower, put on fresh makeup, and donned her afternoon purchases. "Not bad if I say so myself. I'll have to go see that Katherine woman again. Soon."

Angela was the first to arrive at her brother's trailer. Everything was decorated for the impending party, the theme of which appeared to be a Mexican Fiesta. An inflatable giant cactus complete with rosy red blossoms rose high above the boxwoods. Red and green chili pepper lights were strung across the front of the trailer and all around the patio area. A bright yellow piñata donkey stood guard at the front door and the Grecian statue wore a large blue and gold sombrero. All this and it wasn't even Cinco de Mayo.

Tony handed his sister a margarita and started to dish out the guacamole when his neighbors, Steve and Monica Miller, walked up. Just as they began telling Angela that they were an ex-priest and ex-nun who fell in love, gave up their orders, and got married, Gilberto showed up carrying a box of chocolate cannoli. "Thought we might want something chocolate for dessert." How did he know she liked chocolate? She didn't remember telling him.

Katherine Burns, the sales woman who sold Angela the green dress, was close on Gilberto's heels with a shopping bag hanging from one arm and her boyfriend, Ramon Enfante, hanging from the other. "Well, it's a small world after all. Get it? Small World? Disney? Florida?" Her giggle sounded forced.

Ramon introduced himself, "Just call me Mongo." He skillfully burrowed a tortilla chip through the guacamole. The chip didn't break. Angela wondered how he did it.

Flames flared up when Tony threw the steaks on the grill. "Hope everyone's hungry. I've got enough meat here to feed an army."

As if trying to live up to his man-about-town reputation, Gilberto placed his arm around Angela's shoulders just as Mongo and Katherine joined them at the grill.

"You were in the army, weren't you Tony?" Mongo was a Cuban refugee who fought Castro during the Cuban Revolution. His nose was crooked, as if it was once broken in a fight.

"I did my bit for Uncle Sam," replied Tony.

"Is that where you got the tattoos?" Even though Katherine was with Mongo she thought Tony was a good-looking man and she didn't try to hide her admiration.

"Yeah, but we're not here to talk about my tattoos. Everyone? I want you to meet my sister Angela. She just moved here from Indiana. Right now she's house-sitting for Jeff Turner but hopefully she'll like you characters well enough to stick around per-

42

manently."

"How could she not like us?" Gilberto tightened his grip on Angela's shoulder.

Angela wondered if she had said or done anything the night before to make Gilberto think his advances were welcomed. She gracefully wiggled free from his grip and walked over to Steve and Monica, who were helping themselves to softdrinks from the ice chest.

"So, how did you two meet?" She turned her back to Gilberto, hoping he'd take the hint and leave her alone.

"We were both working in Nicaragua," replied Monica. "We were opposed to Somoza's regime and helped organize the Sandinista National Liberation Front that eventually ended his dictatorship." Except for the fact she was wearing a pale pink halter-top and white shorts, Monica had the look of a nun. She didn't smile much, her forehead was deeply furrowed, and her eyes looked like they had seen more than their fair share of war.

"Wow. Sounds dangerous." Angela was amazed that a woman would get involved in something like that. But then, Monica looked tough enough to bring the wrath of God down upon even the most tyrannical despot.

"It was very dangerous. There was fighting everywhere. Innocent women and children were killed, homes were burned to the ground, and cities were bombed. When we went to sleep at night, we were never sure we'd wake up in the morning." Tears glazed Monica's eyes. Did the ex-nun have a soft side?

"I think that's what drew us together." Steve looked into his wife's eyes. His love for her was evident. "We weren't ready to die because we hadn't experienced all that life had to offer." The ex-priest was wearing cutoff jeans and a gray muscle shirt that showcased a few of his finer assets. He was so tan and brawny that Angela had trouble picturing him in clerical clothing. Swim trunks, maybe. But a collar? Never.

"Don't listen to him, Angela. The truth is he was tired of eating his own cooking." Monica poked her husband in the ribs.

"Well yeah, that and a couple other things. You've got to come over some time and try her gallo pinto, Angela." Steve made an "okay" sign with his fingers.

Forcing herself to stop looking at his muscles, Angela managed a weak, "What's that?"

"Just a fancy name for red beans and rice," answered Monica. "But it goes great

44

with barbecued chicken or fish." She wiped a bit of guacamole from her husband's chin.

"Boy, with all the invitations I've been getting, I'm gonna gain twenty pounds if I'm not careful."

"Don't worry, sis. I'll work it off ya." Tony was walking around with an icy pitcher filling up everyone's glasses.

"Did she tell you she'll be working for Tony?" Gilberto wormed his way into the conversation.

"You're going to work for the Bug Assassin?" Steve's smile was almost as broad as his shoulders.

"That's the plan." Angela wished Gilberto was a bug. Maybe then she could get rid of him.

Katherine's shrill voice filled the air. "Hey, Tony. You're not burning those steaks, are you?"

"Oops. Almost forgot." Tony threw back the grill cover just in time to save the steaks from total annihilation. "Everyone wants theirs well done. Right?"

A few steps away, Fran placed a large bowl of Spanish rice, a basket of tortillas, corn on the cob, and a pot of refried beans on the picnic table.

Katherine walked over to check everything out. "What's with the corn, Fran? You know

45

I wear dentures."

"That's why I made the beans," laughed Fran. "They'll hold your teeth in place while you're chomping on the corn. Okay, everyone. Grab a seat. Dinner is served."

For the next thirty minutes, the only words spoken around the long picnic table were "Can you pass the beans, please?" and "Are there more tortillas?"

Angela looked around and realized she'd never run into a more off-the-wall group of people. For starters, there was her ex-paratrooper brother who displayed his tattoos like medals and waged war against unsuspecting bugs. He'd been nice enough to offer her a job and a place to live but ever since she arrived at the party, it felt like he was trying to avoid her — almost as if he didn't want her there.

Then there was that loud-mouthed Katherine and her Cuban boyfriend who followed her around like a lost puppy. Was he hanging on to the redheaded woman for love or money? And what about the priest and nun? What would cause a good-looking man like him to join the priesthood then give it all up for a woman like her? Clearly, it wasn't her sensible shoes or intimidating demeanor.

And, of course, there was that suave Italian. He might have been a good cook and not a bad looker for an old guy but did he think she was attracted to him? The only one in the whole group who seemed halfway normal was her sister-in-law, and sometimes even she acted a bit peculiar.

Once everyone had their fill and Fran stood up to clear the table, Katherine grabbed her shopping bag and officially proclaimed it was "game time."

"Oh, no." The response was unanimous. Everyone knew Katherine specialized in mindless party games. Many an evening had come to an abrupt end when she made her all-too-familiar announcement.

"Come on, everyone. You'll like this one, it's all about baby boomers." She wasn't giving up.

"What do you know about baby boomers, Katherine?" Gilberto was helping Fran with the dishes. "You were born in the thirties."

"Watch it, mister wise guy. I know where you live."

While Tony made the rounds with more drinks, Katherine explained the rules of the game. "It's sort of like Trivial Pursuit. You take a card from the blue deck and try to answer the question. If you get it right, the next person tries and we keep going around until someone misses."

"And den what habbens?" Mongo sounded like he'd had too much to drink.

"Anyone who misses has to take a card from the red deck and do whatever it says."

"Oh, goody." Angela knew where things were going and she wasn't pleased.

"All right, let's give it a try and see what happens." Monica sounded like she might have been a drill instructor in a previous life. "I'll start." She chose a card from the blue deck. It said to name the place where many 1950s teenage dates ended.

"That's too easy," said Monica. "At the submarine races of course."

Steve checked the answer book. "You're right. How did you know that?"

"I was a teenager before I became a nun, sweetie." She laughed but no one joined her.

"Okay. My turn." Steve handed the answer book to Mongo and drew a card. "Who was the first man to run the four-minute mile?"

"Another easy one," he said. "That was Roger Bannister. He ran the mile in three minutes and fifty nine seconds."

"Correcto-mundo," slurred Mongo. "Now it's my turn."

He took a card and read it. "Name Elbis Presley's first hit. *Hound Dog.* Eberyone knows dat. Eben Castro liked it."

"Nope," replied Gilberto. "It was *Heart-*

break Hotel. Now you'll have to take a card from the red deck and do what it tells you to do."

"Are you sure it wasn't *Hound Dog?*" Mongo looked ready to cry.

"Positive. Now just take one of those red cards."

"Okay, okay. Gimme a break." Mongo took a card. It said to stand on one foot and recite *Mary Had a Little Lamb.* Standing up, he raised one foot and attempted to steady himself on the other. "Mary hadda widdle wam, whose feet was widda no, an ebby where dat Mary went the wam was sure to glow." When he started to wobble sideways, he grabbed the Grecian statue. Luckily, Tony saw what was happening and steadied the statue before Mongo could knock it over. The sombrero, however, went flying across the yard.

"Cool it, Mongo. You're tearing the place up." Tony tried to put the sombrero back on the statue but Mongo grabbed it and placed it on his head.

"Oye!" yelled the Cuban. "Les go skinny-dippin."

The inebriated Cuban was coming out of more than just his shell. By the time Katherine reached him, he had his shirt and shoes off and was wrestling with his zipper.

49

About the only thing still in place was the sombrero.

"Yeah, let's do it." Katherine grabbed Mongo by the arm and started to lead him toward the clubhouse.

"Why don't you just take him home, Katherine?" asked Monica. "He could drown in that pool. Besides, I think it's time to call it a night before we all end up making fools of ourselves."

Steve hugged his wife. "Ah, come on, honey. The party is just getting started."

"Did you forget you have to do the readings at church tomorrow morning?" The "don't be stupid look" on Monica's face said more than her words.

"Oh, yeah. Church. Guess you're right. It's past our bedtime." Steve gave Monica a gentle pat on the rump and she gave him one back — only harder.

When all the guests were gone, Fran excused herself and left Tony and Angela with half a pitcher of margaritas and the leftover guacamole.

"Think this stuff is safe to eat?" asked Angela.

"Probably not. Looks kind of green to me." Tony swirled a finger through the guacamole then licked it clean. "So whaddaya think of your new neighbors?"

"Well, they're different. I'll say that for them. I'm glad that stupid game didn't go on for very long, though."

"Why's that? I thought it was kind of funny." Tony took a sip of his drink. He'd downed six or seven that night but they hadn't seemed to affect him.

"I don't think it's very funny making someone do dumb tricks especially when they've had too much to drink." Angela flicked the salt from the rim of her glass.

"Oh, lighten up, sis."

"What's that supposed to mean?"

"It means you need to learn how to enjoy yourself."

"I do enjoy myself." The conversation had taken a wrong turn and Angela was becoming defensive.

"No. You don't. I was watching you tonight. Instead of jumping right in and having some fun you held back and looked like you'd rather be somewhere else."

"I'm sorry, Tony, but that's just the way I am. It takes me a while to warm up to people." She dug a chip into the guacamole. It broke.

"Well, get over it."

"What, and be like your drunken friends? They were acting like a bunch of senior delinquents." She considered mentioning

51

that he had been drinking pretty heavily as well but thought better of it.

"Maybe you could learn a thing or two from them."

"Like what?" She grabbed another tortilla chip and stuffed it in her mouth without dip.

"Like there's a lot more to life than spending all your time worrying about growing old."

Angela wondered why people were always telling her how to live her life. First her parents and teachers, then her ex-husband and that kid down at the store, and now her brother. "I'm not worried about getting old."

"No? Then what are you worried about? Not finding another man?"

"Do I look like I need a man, Tony?"

"Maybe if you had a man in your life you wouldn't act like such a prude."

That did it. Being told she needed a man was bad enough. Being told she acted like a prude was going way too far. "You know something, Tony? I didn't come down here just so you could tell me what I need or how I should act."

"So why did you come?"

"You know why."

"No. I don't. Why don't you tell me?"

"Because my job sucked the life out of me and my landlord said I had to get rid of my dog. I didn't know where else to go." The truth was bitter and she practically spit the words out.

"Oh. So I was your last resort, right? Look Angela, I thought I was doing you a favor by offering you a job and a place to live but you act like it's some kind of punishment."

Tony's words were like a dull knife cutting into Angela's heart. "Eat dirt, Tony. I don't need favors from you or anyone else." She stood up, finished her drink, and slammed the empty glass on the table.

"Hey, you two. Keep it down. People are trying to sleep." Fran was standing in the doorway with a cup of hot chocolate in one hand and a cigarette in the other. Her hair was in green rollers and she was wearing a faded blue bathrobe.

"It's okay, Fran. I was just leaving," replied Angela. Then turning toward her brother, she said, "Maybe moving down here was a mistake."

"Maybe it was," mumbled Tony as she walked away.

4
SUNDAY BLUES

The blinds were drawn, the lights were off, and except for the monotonous whirl of a ceiling fan, the only sound in the small trailer was the persistent click of Gizmo's nails as he wandered around the room and banged into furniture in an effort to wake his mistress. No such luck — she hardly moved. All the drinking the night before had been a bad idea and now she was paying for it. All of a sudden, the phone rang. The blare sent shock waves skyrocketing from the bottom of her skull to the top of her head

"Put your suit on and meet me at the pool." It was Fran.

"Sorry, Fran. I'm not in the mood." The idea of spending time in the sun was out of the question.

"I said meet me at the pool." Even though she was only five-foot-two, Fran had a knack of always getting her way, even if it meant raising her voice a notch or two.

Deciding it was better to obey than pay the inevitable consequences, Angela hung up the phone and started digging through her yet unpacked suitcases. "Why can't everyone just leave me alone?"

It was well past noon by the time she found her bathing suit and made her way to the recreation complex. The wispy clouds hanging high in the pale blue sky did little to block the blazing sun and within minutes the top of her head felt like that proverbial egg on a sidewalk.

"With my luck, I'll probably end up with third degree burns."

The pool was one of those larger-than-life beachfront-entry jobs with waterfalls and palm trees off to one side, a canvas canopy spanning the mid-section, and cushioned chaise lounges positioned wherever room allowed. Several residents were noisily splashing around in the water with their grandchildren and Fran was relaxing on a chaise lounge in the shade.

"Hi, lady. Sorry I took so long. I had a little trouble finding my bathing suit." Angela shuffled toward her sister-in-law.

"Good grief. You look terrible." Fran offered her a bottle of V8.

"I think the guacamole went bad." Angela

took a sip from the bottle and realized it wasn't vegetable juice — it was a Bloody Mary. If there was one thing she didn't need that morning, it was more alcohol. In fact, she didn't care if she ever had it again. She placed the bottle on a table and melted into a lounge next to Fran's.

"Your brother told me what happened last night." Fran tried to look serious.

"Yeah, well, he was being a real jerk." Angela really didn't want to talk about her brother but it looked like Fran wasn't about to let her off the hook.

"Welcome to my world." Fran took a sip from her can of softdrink. Angela wondered if there was rum in it.

"How do you stand it?"

"Actually, that's one of the things that attracted me to him."

"You're kidding, right?" Angela knew the way Tony pushed people around and thought it was strange that Fran found his heavy-handed demeanor appealing.

"No, really. He says what he thinks and he doesn't sugar-coat things just to be politically correct. He tells it like it is and you always know where you stand with him."

"Yeah, I know. He practically told me I was some kind of loser."

"I'm sure that's not what he meant." Fran almost sounded apologetic.

"Well, it sure sounded like it."

"Listen, Angela. Your brother worries about you. He never liked Carl and he was actually happy when you got divorced."

"I'm glad someone was."

Fran twisted in her chair so that she was facing Angela. "Hear me out. When you got divorced, your brother thought things would get better for you. Then you ended up in that hardware store and everything seemed to go from bad to worse. You were working crazy hours, doing physical labor, and you just about gave up dating all together. Tony wanted to help but you were so far away he couldn't do much. That's why he started bugging you about moving down here."

"And we all know how that turned out." Angela was beginning to feel as if she might live. She wondered if that was a good thing.

"You can make it work, Angela."

"I'm not sure I want to."

"At this point, you don't have much choice. You quit your job, sold everything you owned, and pulled up stakes. Looks like you're gonna be here a while."

Fran was right. Angela had given up everything to move to Florida. She had no house, no furniture, no job, and she'd already spent what little money she had. She didn't want to go back to working in a hardware store but she didn't have skills to do anything else. She was stuck and she didn't like it.

"So, now what? I live in a trailer park and kill bugs for the rest of my life?"

"Hey, don't knock it. It's a good life. Living in a trailer doesn't make you trailer trash, and killing bugs certainly doesn't make you the Boston Strangler. Tony and I have met a lot of wonderful people and his work leaves enough free time so we can enjoy them."

Fran sounded so proud of her life that Angela decided not to antagonize her. "I know you're concerned about me and I really appreciate it. It's just that I feel like a fish out of water. I don't know my way around, I don't know anything about the exterminating business, and I don't know what's going to happen next."

"Take it one day at a time. Tony says you'll start training tomorrow morning."

"How long will that take?"

"You can learn the basics in a week and be out on your own in less than a month."

"What do you mean — 'on my own?' "

"Going out on service calls without Tony."

"And what's he gonna be doing while I'm

out on the calls." Angela thought the whole thing was beginning to sound a little fishy. Had he talked her into coming just so he could lay around while she did all the work?

"He wants to spend more time working on advertising and promotion. He says if he can bring in more customers, he'll hire more employees. One day he might even open another office or two."

"He never told me he had such big plans."

"Well, he only started thinking about it recently. I guess your being here has given him some ideas."

"But what if I end up not liking the job? Or what if I decide I don't want to spend the rest of my life in Florida? What will that do to his big plans?"

"Oh, don't worry, Angela. You're gonna like it here. And as far as learning your way around, I'm sure everyone around here will help out. As a matter of fact, Monica called this morning and mentioned you're more than welcome to attend their service tonight."

"What kind of service?"

"Just one of those non-denominational, Sunday get-togethers. There's a lot of singing, some prayers, and Steve usually has a short sermon. It's sort of like a Baptist revival — only shorter. Guess Steve and

Monica never got that religion thing out of their blood. Your brother won't go but I'll keep you company if you want."

"Church really isn't my thing, Fran." It didn't seem like the right time to discuss the fact that she hadn't stepped foot inside a church since her divorce. But then, when would there ever be a right time?

"Oh come on, Angela. Give it a try. There won't be any booze but Monica makes a pretty mean tropical punch."

Angela wondered if she wouldn't be better off staying at home and watching reruns with Gizmo. Maybe even an old *Miami Vice* episode. She'd always loved Don Johnson. But Fran promised the meeting wouldn't last more than an hour, so she agreed to tag along. After all, how bad could it be?

Steve and Monica's trailer was an impressive triple-wide that stretched across two lots around the corner from the clubhouse. A six-inch-tall, white, vinyl picket fence surrounded the pint-sized Kentucky-blue lawn, and a treadmill and exercise bike took center stage in the floor-to-ceiling glass enclosed sunroom. Angela wondered if that was where Steve worked on his magnificent physique. She promised herself to find out.

Fran led the way through a set of lace-covered French doors into a room filled with padded chairs, a banquet table laden with rich-looking desserts, expensive looking religious paintings, and a small podium from which Steve would most likely deliver his sermon. Gilberto and Katherine were already there as were several other people that Angela didn't recognize. Not surprisingly, Mongo was missing.

Looking around, Angela noticed that just about everyone was dressed in shorts, tee shirts, and flip-flops. A few even looked like they'd just come from the pool. Once all the appropriate introductions, hellos, and good to see yous were made, Fran and Angela took their seats and chatted with the people around them until Monica stepped up to the podium and called for everyone's attention.

"I'm glad to see so many familiar faces here again tonight and I'd like to take this opportunity to introduce Egret Cove's newest resident, Angela Dunn. Angela? Could you stand up and tell us a little something about yourself?"

Feeling very much as if she was at an AA meeting, Angela reluctantly obeyed and stood up. "Hi. My name is Angela and I'm a chocoholic."

Laughter filled the room.

She tried to hide her embarrassment and

continued. "Actually, what I meant to say is that I'm originally from Indiana but I came down here to house sit for Jeff Turner and work for my brother Tony. I think you call him the Bug Buster or something like that."

More laughter. Angela felt herself getting in deeper and deeper.

"Anyway, I'll be here for a year and I hope to get to know all of you." Looking like a fifth grader who'd just been reprimanded by her teacher, she hastily sat down and hung her head.

"Thank you, Angela," respond Monica. "I'm sure we're all glad you're here. Now, we will start tonight's service with one of my favorite hymns, *How Great Thou Art,* and then Steve will take over." She had the crowd under her thumb. "Please rise."

Everyone stood up and started to sing. When she ran out of words, Angela starting lip-syncing and wondered how many others in the room were doing the same thing.

By the end of the hymn, Steve was standing at the podium. He wore a pale blue turtleneck. A large ebony cross suspended from a black cord hung around his neck. After reciting a short prayer, he launched into his sermon.

"Most of us lead sheltered lives. We live in a place where everyone is pretty much the same age, where we don't have to worry about crime, and where as Garrison Keillor is fond of saying, 'All the women are strong and the men good-looking.' "

Several people giggled but Steve kept talking.

"Yet there is something dark and evil right outside our door that has the ability to ruin our lives and those of our families." He paused for effect. "It's known as addiction and it comes in many guises. Some people are addicted to alcohol, drugs, gambling, or like Angela, chocolate."

Angela felt everyone's eyes on her. She wondered if she could crawl under her chair.

"Most of us associate family with being there for each other and taking care of each other, however when there is an addict in the family, the family unit can be stretched to the breaking point. In order to draw attention away from himself, the addict often goes to great lengths to offend or alienate other family members."

How could people do things like that to their families?

"The speed with which an individual becomes addicted varies with the substance, the frequency of use, the intensity of pleasure, and the individual's genetic makeup. Some alcoholics report they exhibited alcoholic tendencies from the moment of first intoxication, while most people can drink socially without ever becoming addicted."

Angela wondered if Steve had chosen this particular subject because of Saturday night's party. Even though everyone else, including her, had been hitting the sauce pretty hard, he and Monica had been drinking soft drinks. Monica obviously kept her husband on a short leash. Who could blame her? With muscles like that, most of the women in the park probably chased after him all the time. Add alcohol to the mix, there was no telling what might happen.

Fran noticed that Angela was distracted and gave her a not-so-gentle nudge with her elbow. "Pay attention. It gets better."

"He's already perfect," whispered Angela. Fran just glared at her.

"Aside from the physical and mental damage, addiction has a profound impact on families. Brothers, sisters, children, even grandchildren are frequently caught up in the turmoil that addiction problems inevitably create. Families are always baffled by addicts simply because their behaviors defy reason. Errors in judgment and mistakes are made over and over again in an almost ritualistic fashion. Often denying he or she has a real problem the addict uses and then swears off the offending substance only to return to it all over again. Consequences seem to mean little. Relationships are manipulated with precision by the abuser leaving loved ones feeling useless, confused or angry."

Tony was a manipulator. Did drinking drive him to it?

"Addicted persons are very impulsive and impatient people who display unpredictable moods and actions that tend to menace those around them. They are very often charming when it counts and abusive when charming doesn't work. They are proficient blame shifters ever rationalizing, intellectualizing, and justifying their position to throw others off balance. They often go through friendships by exploiting others until destruction of the relationship occurs. When faced with the ultimate consequences of their actions, they explode in anger."

Maybe that was why Tony always seemed so edgy.

"Living with an addict can be a traumatic experience with many ups and downs occurring in the daily routine. There are feelings of anger, confusion, desperation, guilt, shame, and helplessness. Family members constantly worry about what will happen next. They suffer from anxiety, depression, digestive problems and re-occurring head-aches. Through fear, shame and embarrass-ment of revealing the addict, they start to withdraw from society. Friends stop visit-ing, hobbies get forgotten, and the addict and his family become more and more iso-lated."

It was all too clear. Tony had a problem. The only reason he gave her a job was so he would have more time to devote to drink-ing. How could she have been so gullible? What could she do now that she knew?

Angela tuned out the rest of Steve's sermon, but afterwards, while everyone else walked over to the dessert table, she hung back to talk to him.

"It's good to see you again, Angela. What did you think of my talk?"

"Well, to tell the truth, Steve, it was a little too depressing for me."

"It should be, Angela. Addiction isn't something to be taken lightly."

Angela wanted to talk to Steve about Tony but Katherine jumped in and tried to take over the conversation.

"Oh, come on, Steve, enough of the sermons. Surely you've got better things to talk about."

"Yes, like maybe the Miami Heat?" Gilberto joined the small group gathering around Steve. He handed Angela a cup of punch and a plate with two chocolate macaroons and a chocolate brownie. She sipped the punch. Fran was right. It was delicious.

Katherine stood on her tiptoes and tried to look Gilberto in the eyes. "The only thing that interests you about the Heat is the cheerleaders."

"You mean the Golden Oldies?" Steve appeared to be enjoying the friendly banter.

"Now, who in their right mind would want to watch a bunch of old women cavorting around a basketball court in gold lamé miniskirts?" Katherine shook her head in disapproval.

"Would red be better?" Gilberto raised his eyebrows.

"Of course — it's my color of choice."

Up until that moment, Angela hadn't realized Katherine had been wearing red every time she'd seen her. Even her hair was red. Once she started to think about it, it made her wonder. "Why red, Katherine?"

Fran stepped in alongside Angela. "Come on, Katherine," she laughed. "We all know you're dying to talk about it so why don't you just tell us . . . what's with all the red?"

"Well, everyone knows I'm president of

the Foxy Ladies," she replied indignantly.

"What are the Foxy Ladies?" It was all new to Angela and for some strange reason she wanted to know more.

"You don't know?" asked Gilberto. "They are a group of over-aged women who get together, wear loud colors, and carry on ridiculous rituals."

"They're not ridiculous and we're not over-aged. We're just a group of good looking ladies who consider themselves foxes. Some, like me, are red foxes, some are silver or blonde, and one is even blue. We all like wearing bright colors and doing fun things." Katherine glared at Gilberto.

"Like what?" asked Angela.

"Well, let's see. We paint our toenails to match our clothes, we have pajama parties, we go on trips, we take belly-dancing classes, and we laugh a lot. Like Emeril says, we 'kick it up a notch.' "

"And that is not childish?" mocked Gilberto.

"Don't listen to him, Angela. Just the fact that women our age are so active makes some people wonder what we're up too. We've even been accused of whipping up secret potions in our kitchens and keeping company with sorcerers."

"That's so bizarre." Angela was suddenly

happy she'd come to the meeting. It was turning out to be a lot more interesting than staying home and watching reruns.

"One of those sorcerers is a guy who lives a couple streets over," added Steve. "I've seen him at several of Katherine's parties. He does all sorts of peculiar things. I heard he was even arrested once for feeding stray cats to alligators. No telling what else he's been up to." Steve curled his fingers, stuck both of his hands in the air, and growled.

"Stop that, Steve. You are going to scare Angela." Gilberto was trying to take control of the situation but Katherine wouldn't let him.

"Seriously, Angela. We're just a bunch of in-our-prime ladies who haven't relegated ourselves to growing old. At least not gracefully. There'll be time enough for that down the road. Meanwhile, we've still got a lot of life in our old bones and we aim to use it. You should join us some time. I think you'd really enjoy yourself."

Not if my life depended on it, thought Angela.

5
ON THE JOB

It was almost ten when Tony banged on his sister's kitchen door. "Come on lazy bones, rise and shine. It's time to get to work."

Angela appeared in the doorway with her hair twisted into a tight braid, a purple bandana tied around the neck of her sweatshirt, steel-toed work boots on her feet, and a pair of gray canvas gloves hanging from the back pocket of her jeans. "Way ahead of you big brother. I've been up for hours. Whatcha think?" She assumed the Vanna pose.

Tony inspected his sister's getup and laughed. "What are you dressed for? Mountain climbing?"

"Well, I thought I might have to do some crawling around so I dressed appropriately. Did I forget anything?" She shot her brother a toothy grin.

"You're not going to crawl under anything until you know what you're doing. That means following me around for a week or two, watching what I do and how I do it, and above all, staying out of trouble."

"Oh, yes sir. Just like the old days when you tried to teach me how to ride a bicycle. Remember that?"

One thing about Tony — he never gave up. Angela couldn't have been more than six years old when she got her first bicycle but she was a little on the chubby side and had a lot of trouble keeping her balance. Their father worked two jobs and their mother was sick so Tony took on the job of teaching his sister how to ride. He held the bike upright, waited until she got settled on the narrow seat and then propelled her and the bicycle around the neighborhood. Every time he took his hands off the bike, Angela fell. She scrapped her knees and elbows, she banged her head on a low-hanging tree limb, and once she even ran into a parked car. It was a disaster and Tony yelled a lot but he never gave up. It took a full summer but by the time school opened, Angela could ride her bicycle.

"Quit lolly-gagging and listen to me. Pest control is a serious business and if you don't know what you're doing you're gonna get hurt."

"Like how?"

"Like breathing toxic fumes, mishandling corrosive chemicals, or having a termite infested house fall on your head."

"You're kidding. Right?" Angela lost her grin.

"It could happen. So pay attention and don't do anything or talk to anyone unless I say it's okay. And if anyone asks, just say you're a technician in training. Got it?"

"Got it. How long will this training thing take?"

"Depends on how fast you learn. Could be a week or two, could be a couple of months. Once I think you know what you're doing you'll be able to work on your own. And after a couple years experience you can apply for certification."

"Couple of years? I thought it was only a couple of months." The sooner she could be on her own, the better. Maybe then she could get away from Tony and go to work for someone else.

"Well, some guys do it quicker than others."

"You mean it'll take longer because I'm a woman?"

"It might." Tony turned and walked toward his truck.

Angela wanted to tell her brother to take a flying leap into the nearest ocean but she held back. She needed to learn this stuff if she wanted to keep on eating. In the meantime, she'd have to swallow her pride and keep her mouth shut.

Tony rolled down the truck window and yelled at his sister. "Come on, let's get going. We've got two appointments this morning and one this afternoon."

"Okay, I'll be right there." After checking to make sure Gizmo had enough toys and water, Angela dashed toward the truck and jumped in.

Their first stop was at a rundown mobile home park a couple miles down the road. Shanty-like trailers, probably evicted from Egret Cove, lined the narrow gravel streets. Worn out trucks and cars covered in rust, bird droppings, and spider webs perched precariously on cinder blocks. Derelict toilets and bathtubs littered what once may have passed as lawns and an unidentifiable odor permeated the air.

"What's that smell?" Angela wrinkled her nose.

"You don't want to know."

Tony pulled up to a trailer that looked like it had been through a war. Windows were busted out, the rickety stairs looked like they wouldn't support a chihuahua, and someone — probably vandals — had bombarded the trailer's pock-marked aluminum walls with paintballs.

"We're not going in are we?" She wanted to be any place but there.

"Sure. I want you to meet someone." He walked into the trailer without knocking. An old woman sat in a tattered Barcalounger drinking something from a caffeine-stained plastic mug. She wore a tin foil cap on her head and combat boots on her feet.

"Hi Gramma. It's me, Tony. Is George around?"

"He went to the store to buy more foil. I want him to cover the windows." Her nicotine-coated gums filled the void where teeth had once been.

"Why? Are they coming in through the windows now?"

"Yes. Two of 'em got in last night and tried to grab me. I knew they wanted to take me back to their ship so I fought them off and yelled for George. Once he came in they ran off."

"Their ship?" Angela wondered if the woman was talking about space aliens.

"Who's that?" The old woman suddenly looked frightened.

"Don't worry, Gramma. That's my sister Angela. She just started to work for me."

"Well you tell her to watch out for THEM. They like pretty young things like her."

"Why don't you tell her what to look for, Gramma. That way she'll know." Tony grinned, crossed his arms, and leaned against the linoleum-covered countertop.

The old woman looked around then, as if to keep others from hearing, began to whisper. "First you'll see the streaks in the sky. Some people say they're contrails but I know better. Those streaks come from spaceships, not airplanes. They're dumping chemicals on us to make us sick. Then you'll hear a buzzing noise in your ears — that's the way they communicate with each other. It gets louder the closer they come. Once they've been in your house, you'll never be able to keep them out, and once they've tagged you, you'll never be able to run from them."

"Have you been tagged?" Angela didn't know whether or not to believe the woman.

"Oh yes. Several times. Here. See these marks on my arms? That's from them. And this one above my ear? That's from them, too."

"Do you know where they come from?"

"Of course I do. The government sends them. And the Vatican, too."

"Why?" The old woman probably thought

Elvis was still alive and out there somewhere.

"Because they want to control us."

"Does the tin foil keep them away?" Angela swallowed a giggle.

"Most of the time but I think I'm going to have to find something stronger because they keep finding ways to sneak in. I just don't know what I'll do if they take me up in their ship."

"Don't worry about that, Gramma. I'm sure George will figure something out. In the meantime, do you mind if we walk around and spray your baseboards?" Tony seemed ready to get out of there.

"Go ahead, Tony. That'll keep them out until George gets back. They don't like the smell you know."

Back in the truck, Angela laughed so hard she almost cried. "I don't believe it. Was that woman for real?"

"Of course she was. That's what happens to people when they get old. They start seeing and hearing things — even little green men."

"Yeah, but what about those marks?" Angela was sure aliens hadn't caused the marks but she had to ask the question anyway.

"Fleas."

"Fleas?"

"Yup. She feeds all the stray cats and lets them come in at night. Everyone has tried to stop her but she says the cats are her only friends. So rather than argue with her, we just all let her have her way and I spray the trailer twice a month."

"I won't have to go in there alone. Will I?"

"You might. But you'll get used to it. It's all part of the job."

On the way to their next appointment, Tony explained that aside from locating and destroying bugs and spiders, a big part of his job was repelling all sorts of other pests including raccoons, bats, and poisonous lizards. "The more we keep away, the less work we have to do."

"What about alligators?" Angela had heard that the reptilian monsters were capable of biting off a human's arm or leg.

"I usually leave gators and snakes to the trappers. A couple of years back the Everglades got overrun with Burmese pythons and the wildlife guys had to go in and clear them out."

"Pythons? They're not native to Florida are they?" Great — something else to worry about.

"No. But a lot of people raise them as pets and then turn them loose in the 'Glades when they get too big to feed or handle. All you need is for two of them to get together and you end up with a whole horde. The wildlife service wanted to set out stuff that would sterilize the snakes but everyone argued that even if the snakes didn't breed, they could still kill pets and other animals so the trappers tried to catch as many as possible."

"Did they get them all?"

"Like I said, all you need is two."

Angela thought it was kind of strange that Tony had chosen a line of work that put him in direct contact with snakes. When they were kids, rather than admitting he was too chicken to walk through grass more than an inch high, he conned his parents into thinking cutting grass was girl's work and Angela ended up with lawnmower duty. When she was no more than nine or ten, she accidentally chopped a snake to pieces with the lawnmower.

With tears streaming from her eyes, she picked up what was left of the reptile, buried it in the vegetable garden, and made up her mind to become a veterinarian so that she could help injured animals. She checked out books from the library, studied dog and cat anatomy, and even volunteered at a local pet shop. Once she realized she might have to cut into an animal to help it, she gave the whole idea up.

Tony had called her gutless. But who was he to talk? He was the one who was afraid of snakes. Not her. And from what Fran said, things hadn't changed much. Tony still wouldn't cut grass, and leaving gators and snakes up to the wildlife service sounded like he'd never gotten over his irrational fears.

"Hey — quit daydreaming," barked Tony, "we've still got work to do."

It was almost noon when they pulled into the parking lot of a New York–style deli. Angela envisioned sinking her teeth into a steaming hot Ruben piled high with sauerkraut and smothered in mozzarella cheese but the vision vaporized when Tony handed her a box of flyers and told her to go in and give it to the cashier. "They stick the flyers in the carry out bags and I give them a discount on roach control."

"They have a roach problem?" Suddenly, the Ruben didn't sound all that appetizing.

"Most restaurants do. That's why I don't eat out much. We're just about through for the morning. Our afternoon appointment is back at the park so I'll make us something to eat when we get back there."

First aliens and now cockroaches. What

next? She took the box and trudged across the parking lot.

The restaurant was just what Angela had expected. Peroxide-blonde waitresses in pink uniforms and white aprons bustled back and forth between crowded booths and tables and shouted orders to cooks secreted away behind a high counter. "Gimme a cowboy with bullets and a Jack Benny to walk." Busboys noisily shuffled soiled plates and flatware onto metal carts as two cashiers rang up diner's bills and processed credit cards. Above all the hullabaloo, a grease-spattered radio blared Chuck Berry's *Blueberry Hill.*

Cockroaches or not, the smells wafting in from the kitchen made Angela's mouth water. She wished she could stay and grab a quick lunch but, looking out the window, she spotted Tony drumming his fingers on the steering wheel. Judging from the expression on his face, she knew it would be better if she came back when she was alone, or at least not with her ill-tempered brother.

On the way back to the trailer park, Tony asked Angela what she wanted for lunch. "Peanut butter or bologna?"

"Neither one but Fran packed the cabinets with food. How about I make us some tuna salad sandwiches and French onion soup?"

"What do you put in your tuna salad?"

"The usual. Mayo, relish, onions, and celery."

"Throw in some jalapeños and it's a deal."

"Anything you want, big brother."

While Angela heated the soup and mixed the tuna salad, Tony sat on the living room floor and played with Gizmo who rolled over and begged to have his tummy scratched.

"Speaking of fleas, did you know your dog has them?"

"Are you sure it isn't just dirt?"

"I've been an exterminator long enough to know fleas when I see them. Where have you been walking him?"

"I didn't like the looks of that dog walking area so I've been taking him down to the open field at the far end of the park."

"Super. That's the one place I don't spray. Now we're going to have to fumigate the trailer, spray around the outside, and dust the dog. Do you have him on any kind of flea and tick program?"

"Well, sure. But it's November, for Pete's sake. All the bugs in Indiana are dead by September."

"Well, we don't get hard freezes down here so fleas and ticks multiply like rabbits.

You'll have to have him on something year round."

"Great." She threw an extra helping of jalapeños into the salad and then placed it, half a loaf of seven-grain bread, and two bowls of steaming soup on the table. "Soup's on."

Tony pulled up a chair, made himself a sandwich, and took a big bite. "Not bad. Needs more jalapeño, but it'll do."

She couldn't win.

Angela decided it was as good a time as any to bring up the subject they'd both been avoiding all morning. "Listen, Tony. About Saturday night . . ."

"Don't worry, little sister. You got a little drunk and said some things you didn't mean." Tony blew on his soup.

"I got drunk?" Was she hearing right?

"Well, I sure didn't."

That was just the problem. Tony had had a lot to drink that night but he wasn't drunk. Not even close. He knew exactly what he was saying and he meant every word of it. He told Angela that she was an old stick-in-the-mud and that she needed to get a life. Now he was acting like he hadn't said anything wrong. Who was he to tell her how to live her life? Was his so perfect?

"Yeah, well, I'm sorry if I said anything

out of line." It took everything she had to get the words out.

"Apology accepted. Just don't let it happen again."

After lunch, Angela and Tony drove over to Gilberto's trailer to check out a hornet's nest rapidly taking over his storage shed.

"Today's Monday so Gil's probably not home."

"How do you know that?" Angela wondered if her brother was familiar with the comings and goings of all his neighbors.

"He's never home on Mondays. Or Thursdays for that matter."

"Why not?"

"I don't know. I never asked him. Maybe he has a girlfriend."

Two or three was more like it. Angela wondered which one he visited on Monday and which one on Thursday.

"Okay. Now before we start, you need to know something about hornets. First off, they're dangerous. Secondly, they're dangerous. And lastly, they're dangerous. When I open the shed door, some of them will fly out. Just stay out of their way and you'll be okay."

"Shouldn't we be wearing protective clothing?" She'd watched enough *Animal Planet* to know that bee people always wore

83

white suits and veiled headgear.

"You've been watching too much television."

See? She was right.

"Once all the hornets fly out, I'll go in and spray the nest. Then we'll come back in a couple of hours, take the nest down, and spray the whole area so they don't come back. That should take care of the problem."

Angela wanted to see exactly how Tony handled the situation so she moved in close behind him and peered over his shoulder. When he opened the shed door, a bunch of hornets flew out just as he had predicted. Tony had performed this exercise so many times he knew to duck before the hornets spotted him but it was all new to Angela and her face must have looked like a giant target because the aggravated hornets aimed straight for it. One landed on her nose and another on her lower lip. Luckily, the bandana protected her neck but, because the gloves were still hanging from her back pocket, several landed on her bare hands.

When she started to scream, Tony whipped around and yelled at her. "I thought I told you to stay out of their way. Did any of them sting you?"

"I think they all did. I feel like a porcupine."

"Here. Lemme see." Tony grabbed Angela's chin and twisted her head from left to right. "They got you, all right. Do you have tweezers back at your trailer?"

"Just the ones I use on my eyebrows."

"That'll do."

Back at the trailer, Tony used the tweezers to pull the stingers from his sister's battered face and hands. When she suddenly pleaded for him to stop, he asked why.

"I don't feel so good. I think my tongue is swelling up and I feel kinda dizzy."

"Quick. Get in the truck. We're going to the emergency room."

6
SICK DAYS

"Knock, knock. It's Katherine. Anyone home?"

"Come on in, Katherine. I'm on the couch." Angela didn't feel like getting up for anyone let alone Katherine. Her hands itched, her lower lip felt like she'd just had Botox, and her nose looked like the rubber bulb off a kid's tricycle horn. Katherine was pleasant enough but with all the medication she was taking, Angela wasn't sure how long she could handle the redhead's exuberance.

"Fran told me you had an accident." Katherine placed a basket of red grapefruits on the kitchen counter.

"News travels fast around here doesn't it?" Angela raked her fingers through her hair trying to push the strays into place.

"Oh yeah, especially when it's something like this. What'd the doctors say?"

"I had some sort of allergic reaction to the hornet stings. I guess my blood pressure dropped pretty low and I was having trouble breathing. They gave me a shot and kept me overnight to make sure my airway didn't close up."

"Same thing happened to Frank, my third husband. He got bit by a honey bee and ended up going into anaphylactic shock."

"Yeah, that's what the doctors called it. Said it could actually be life threatening."

"Frank got so sick it affected his heart. Six weeks later he had a heart attack and went belly up."

"Wow. From just one bee bite? That's terrible. Guess I got off lucky." Getting fifteen hornet bites was far better than getting fitted for wings and a halo.

"So what kind of drugs did they give you? Anything good?"

"No, just some antihistamines and a hydrocortisone cream. The doctor told me to stay off my feet for a couple of days until I feel stronger so Tony said I could take the rest of the week off."

"He's such a sweetie."

"Yeah — a real gem." Angela was in no mood to talk about her brother. "So tell me, Katherine, how many times have you been married?"

"At last count?" Katherine ticked the number off on her flawlessly polished scarlet nails. "Five. Three died, one moved in with a South Beach waiter, and one joined the Foreign Legion or something equally ridiculous."

"Are you planning on marrying Mongo?"

"I don't know yet. I like him well enough but he's big-time into politics and I'm not sure I could handle a steady diet of that. He's Cuban, you know."

"Yes, I know." Had she forgotten they were all at the same party?

"Cubans are very passionate about their country and women." Katherine's eyes glistened with excitement.

"You and Mongo don't still . . . you know . . . do you?"

"Make whoopee? Sure we do. Why not?"

"Oh . . . I don't know. Maybe because you're a little old for that sort of thing?"

"You'd be surprised what a little Viagra can do, Angela. Besides, being in love isn't just for the young. It's like I was telling you the other night at Steve's. The most important thing about life is to enjoy it as long and as often as possible. Speaking of which, I've got a couple of days off. How 'bout you and me take a ride down to my condo in Key West tomorrow?"

"I'm not sure that would be a good idea what with all the medication I'm taking."

She was about to add that she'd just as soon stay home and watch Jerry and Oprah but Katherine cut her off.

"We'll take the drugs with us. I'll do all the driving and you can just lean back and enjoy the scenery. We'll stop for lunch at one of those seaside joints and we'll have dinner at Sloppy Joe's. It's the hottest place in town. Sound like fun?"

"What about Gizmo?" Maybe that would get her off the hook.

"Mongo can take care of him."

"I probably shouldn't." Angela tried to look sick.

"I'll pick you up tomorrow at nine. Is that too early?"

"No . . . but . . ."

"No more buts. I'll see you in the morning so be ready. Oh, and by the way, I drive a convertible so bring a hat and lots of sunscreen."

Even though the idea of spending two days with a Lucille Ball look-alike didn't make Angela want to turn somersaults, the thought of spending those days in Key West did. She'd always wanted to see the Keys but all her previous visits to Florida had been short and there was never enough time to drive all the way down to the remote islands. This time, she had all the time in the world and considering what she'd been through the last couple of days, she felt like she deserved a little R&R. She could kick back, get some sun, and probably eat some good food. Of course, going away meant packing an overnight bag and the last time she looked, all of her suitcases, including half of what was in them, lay scattered across her bedroom floor. It was time she got her act together.

It took almost two hours to unpack and arrange all her clothes in the small walk-in closet but once she was done, Angela stood back and admired her work. "See Gizmo? Now I can find what I'm looking for. Pretty neat. Huh?" The dog just glared at her with a reproachful, "Where's my stuff?" look.

After a quick lunch, Angela plopped back on the couch. "Time for a nap, boy. Wanna join me?" She and the dog curled up under a light afghan and within minutes the room was filled with snores and snorts. Two hours later there was another knock at the door.

"Now, what?" She threw the afghan to the floor, stumbled toward the door, stubbed her toe on an end table, and muttered a few well-chosen expletives as she opened the door.

Gilberto stood in the doorway carrying what appeared to be a very hot covered dish. "I just took this lasagna out of the oven and thought you might like to share it with me. But if this is a bad time, I can come back later."

"No, it's nothing. I just stubbed my toe. Come on in. If that lasagna tastes half as good as it smells, I'll eat the whole thing myself."

Angela led Gilberto into the kitchen and threw together a quick salad while he rummaged around, found some forks and dishes, and set them out on the table.

"How are you feeling, Angela?" He moved around the small kitchen as if it were his own.

"Pretty good, actually. Katherine came by this morning and invited me to go to Key West tomorrow."

"To her condo?"

"Yes. Have you been there?"

"Several times. It is quite lovely." Gilberto slicked back his meticulously groomed silver hair.

She should have known. Of course he'd been to Katherine's condo. Why not? After all, he was the senior Don Juan of the trailer park. Wasn't he?

"How long will you be there?"

"Just overnight. Katherine said something about going to Sloppy Joe's for dinner.

That's one of Hemingway's old haunts isn't it?"

"Yes, it is. But I hear it can be a pretty rough place. I really don't think two women should go there alone."

Angela wondered if Gilberto was trying to wrangle an invitation. "Oh, we'll be okay. But I'll take my pepper spray . . . just in case."

"Nevertheless, Angela, be careful. Katherine has been known to get a little wild down there. I wouldn't want you getting hurt or anything."

"Don't worry about me, Gilberto. I'll be fine." Angela shoved a forkful of the lasagna in her mouth. The cheese melted on her tongue and the delicately spiced sauce quickly washed it down. She wondered if the man's success with women had anything to do with his cooking abilities.

The next morning Katherine and Mongo showed up bright and early. Katherine's "convertible" turned out to be a 1967 VW Beetle with mag wheels, twin polished chrome tail pipes, and a Mercedes grill. Naturally, the top was down and, even more naturally, the tricked-out car was painted red.

After Angela showed Mongo where she kept Gizmo's food and leash, Katherine carried her overnight bag to the car. When Angela noticed how small her case was in comparison to Katherine's, she began to worry. "I hope we're not going anywhere fancy. I didn't bring much."

"No problem. All you'll need down there is a Jantzen and a smile. I brought my biggest suitcase so I could load it up with piña colada mixings. Don't want to run out. Do we?"

Angela was beginning to understand what Gilberto had been warning her about. Maybe Katherine was one of those dark and evil things Steve talked about on Sunday night and maybe their little road trip would turn into a twenty-four hour binge. Then what would she do?

"Well come on girl," shouted Katherine. "Let's get this show on the road. We're losing daylight."

About an hour south of Miami, the little red car pulled into a Holiday Inn parking lot. The lot was filled with cars, most with Florida license plates but a few with Georgia and Alabama tags.

"What are we stopping here for?" Angela was in a hurry to get to Key West but if Katherine kept stopping every hour, it would be dark before they got there.

"There's something you've got to see.

Come on." Katherine was out of the car before Angela could object.

"We're in Key Largo right now. Up ahead is a place where you can swim with dolphins and beyond that is a coral reef where they have an awesome underwater hotel. Mongo and I were going to stay there once but he chickened out at the last minute. Said he was afraid of leaks so we came back here and discovered this."

"What?" Angela had to run to keep up with Katherine. Did the woman never stop?

"It's the boat from *The African Queen.* Most of the movie was filmed on a phony Hollywood set but the boat's the real thing. The guy who owns the hotel bought it and he takes people out on excursions. Check it out."

Katherine and Angela walked around, ran their hands across the boat's wooden hull, and wondered what it was like riding down the river with a ne're-do-well riverboat pilot. Bogart sure looked scruffy. Did he smell as bad as he looked? What if Hepburn needed a potty break? Did Bogie pull over to the side of the river and mutter, "Here's looking at you, Kid?" Hopefully not. Anyway, that was a different movie. Wasn't it?

Snippets from the movie played in Angela's mind and she wanted to see how

Katherine Hepburn must have felt standing on the windswept deck. "Can we get on?"

"Why not? What's the worst they can do? Ask us to leave?"

They took their shoes off, climbed on board, and took pictures of each other pretending to pull up the anchor and hoist the sail. While clowning around and doing a little cheesecake on the deck, they spotted a security guard headed their way. They hurriedly jumped off the boat, grabbed their shoes, and ran for the car. Once safely on the road, Katherine filled Angela in on the agenda for the rest of the day.

"We'll stop for lunch in Islamorada and then if you feel up to it, we can see if we can get into the Turtle Hospital." She was full of ideas.

"Turtle Hospital?"

"Yeah. It's a place where they take injured sea turtles, rehabilitate them, and then turn them back into the ocean."

"Cool. But what did you mean . . . if we can get in?"

"They like people to make reservations in advance but I know the guy who runs the place so I'm sure we'll get in."

"Oh. Okay. But let's have lunch first. I'm starving." Angela wasn't sure if it was the hothouse atmosphere or the change of scenery. Either way, since moving to Florida her appetite had just about doubled what it was in Indiana. If she wasn't careful, she'd end up looking like a manatee.

"Me, too. The restaurant's just down the road a bit. We'll be there in a jiffy."

Katherine waved at a couple teenage hitchhikers as she sped past them. She probably would have picked them up if her car had been bigger or if Angela hadn't been along. Thank God for small blessings.

A few minutes later, Katherine parked the ersatz Mercedes in front of what she referred to as her favorite "cheesy roadside café." A crumbling whitewashed wall surrounded a small patio where several 1950s-style metal lawn chairs, sorely in need of fresh paint, waited in anticipation of the impending tourist onslaught. Just beyond the dimly lit interior dining room, another patio spread out across a sprawling white sand beach.

"Wow. There's nothing cheesy about that view." Angela couldn't believe her eyes. She'd seen the ocean before but never like this. The horizon fell off into blue-gray water that seemed to go on forever. Off in the distance a freighter silently chugged away to exotic ports. Close to shore boisterous seagulls circled above palatial yachts and wave runners trailed rooster tails in their wake. She wanted to kick her shoes off and run in the waves but thought better of it. After all, she had to uphold her brother's fuddy-duddy image of her.

A young girl led the women to an ocean front table, left two menus, and said that a waiter would be by shortly to take their order but Katherine was too busy to look at the menu. "Hey, check out the buns on that waiter." She nodded her head toward the young man.

"Katherine, behave yourself. You're embarrassing me." Angela was wearing sunglasses but she lowered them enough to get a good look. "Hmmm. You're right. Wonder if he works out?"

The women giggled like schoolgirls when the waiter came by to take their order and they were still at it when he brought their food. From the grin on his face, he seemed to know what they were laughing about. And he seemed to enjoy their attention. Maybe his looks helped him get bigger tips.

It struck Angela how fortunate she was to be in a place where she could just hop in her car and run down to the Keys whenever she wanted. The sun was relaxing, the food was delicious, and the views were beyond incredible. What more could anyone want?

She laid her fork down and looked out across the ocean. "This place is wonderful."

"Isn't it? I always stop here whenever I go down to the condo."

"How often is that?"

"Like everything else in my life — not often enough."

"You really enjoy yourself, don't you Katherine." The mood at the table suddenly turned serious.

"Well, sure. Don't you?"

"My brother doesn't think so." She barely whispered the words.

"What makes you say that?"

"Because he told me so." Angela fought to keep her tears back.

"Oh, I'll bet he was just teasing you."

"No, he wasn't." What would it take to make this woman understand? Did she have to draw pictures?

"What did he say?"

"Basically that I wouldn't recognize fun if it walked up and hit me over the head."

"No!" Concern spread across Katherine's face.

"Yes. And he also said that I probably shouldn't have moved down here."

"When did he say that?"

"Saturday night. Right after the party. We got into this big argument and he just flew off the handle. It got so bad that Fran had to come out and tell us to shut up."

"I can't believe it. That's so unlike Tony."

Katherine didn't seem willing to accept the fact that Tony could be cruel and heartless. It probably had something to do with his drinking but Angela wasn't about to discuss her brother with a woman who had a suitcase full of piña colada mixings.

"Well, believe it because it's true."

"So, what are you gonna do?"

"I'm not sure." Angela looked back toward the ocean.

"Well, I've got an idea or two."

"Like what?"

A mischievous grin spread across Katherine's face. "You'll see, girlfriend. You'll see."

7
ON THE BEACH

The sign on the front door of the Turtle Hospital stated, "Closed — Out on Rescue."

"Well, darn," groaned Katherine. "I really wanted you to see this place. Guess we're gonna have to stop on the way back."

"Think they'll be back by then?" Angela thought it was strange that everyone was gone but then maybe they only had a few people on staff and needed every available body whenever there was an emergency.

"Who knows? They're such a strange bunch they might be gone for the rest of the week."

Was the woman who drove a Mercedes wannabe, wore nothing but red and purple clothing, and painted her fingernails like circus posters calling other people *strange?* Obviously, she hadn't looked in a mirror lately. If she had, she might have noticed she could qualify for Queen of the Weird.

"Well, never mind." Katherine quickly

ushered Angela back to the car. "This'll give us time for a swim. You brought your suit didn't you?"

"My Jantzen AND my smile." As proof, Angela grinned like Alice's Cheshire cat.

"Good girl. Let's hit the road. Again."

Angela was afraid her traveling companion was about to belt out Willie Nelson's annoying road song but, luckily, she just hopped in the car, started the engine, and announced: "Next stop Key West." Thank goodness for small favors.

The condo was an oceanfront, five-story, white brick building that sat less than a block from the famous Mallory Square where tourists gathered every evening to watch the sun sink into the Gulf of Mexico. According to Katherine, it was one of the best shows in town but if Angela wasn't up to being jostled around by crowds, they could watch the sunset from the condo balcony.

"Let's play it by ear." As far as Angela was concerned, she would just as soon spend the whole evening cooped up at the condo.

"Whatever you decide is fine with me," replied Katherine. "In the meantime, let's get our suits on and check out the action down at the pool."

If that didn't sound like trouble, nothing

did. But Angela didn't say anything. Maybe no one else would be down at the pool. After all, it was the heat of the afternoon and most people were probably running around doing tourist things or chilling out somewhere that had air-conditioning.

Before Angela could look around the condo and get her bearings, Katherine appeared in the doorway wearing a red fifties-style Ester Williams bathing suit and carrying a tote bag and two very large, very fluffy beach towels — one red and one purple. "You're not changed," she scolded. "Time's a-wasting, Angela. Hustle your bustle."

Hustle your bustle? Where'd she come up with that? An old police Gazette? "Speaking of bustles, you look great in that suit Katherine. How do you keep your shape?"

"Oh, you know. A little nip, a little tuck. It's amazing what they can do nowadays. Now hurry up, we're losing the sun."

Angela got into her swimsuit, looked in the mirror, and sighed. "Guess we know who'll win this beauty contest." She grabbed a bath towel from the bathroom rack, wrapped it around her body, and headed for the door where Katherine was waiting.

"Nice towel," snickered Katherine. "I'll race you to the elevator."

Several rows of unoccupied deck chairs

surrounded the diamond-shaped pool whose water was bluer than the ocean that lay just beyond. As Angela predicted, there wasn't another soul around but she quickly realized it wasn't because they were out doing tourist things — it was because the water in the pool was well over ninety degrees. You could get heat stroke just looking at it. Angela was so afraid of ending up like Katherine's third husband that she didn't even want to stick her toe in the water. "We're not going in — are we?"

"Of course not," Katherine assured her. "That water could cook a lobster in two minutes flat. We'll just hang out down here a while and see if anything good turns up." She pulled a plastic tube from the tote and rubbed suntan lotion on her arms and legs. "Want some?"

Angela shook her head and adjusted her sunglasses. It was three in the afternoon but the sun's glare off the water made her squint. "What time does that sunset thing start?"

"Around six but people start gathering as early as four."

"Just to watch the sun go down?"

"Oh, no. There's a lot more to it than that. They've got at least a dozen bars set up along the beach, there's lots of food carts, and there are fire eaters, jugglers, and all sorts of musicians everywhere you look. It's got a real South American *Carnaval* atmosphere."

"Wow." Angela thought it all sounded pretty wild but this was Florida and maybe that was the way they did things down here.

After forty minutes of baking in the scorching sun and encountering only two teenage boys (too young even for Katherine) the women folded their blankets and headed back towards the elevator. "Maybe we'll have better luck tonight," chuckled Katherine.

Dreading having to take part in the hedonistic ritual, Angela muttered a quiet, "One can only hope," and slouched into the back corner of the elevator. She was beginning to think that coming on this trip had been a bad idea and that Gilberto's warnings had been right on target. But it was too late. She was already there and except for hitchhiking all the way back to Egret Cove, she had no way to get home. Since it was only for one night, she decided she might just as well go down to the beach, see what all the fuss was about, and then have a nice dinner somewhere. If Katherine acted up or things got out of hand, she could fake a headache and go back to the condo — even if she had to go alone.

Angela took a fast shower, washed the sweat from her hair, and slipped into a yellow tank top and a pair of white pedal pushers. Or did they call them clam diggers down here? Looking in the mirror, she noticed her cheeks and nose were sunburned so she smeared on a generous layer of zinc oxide. Then, almost as an afterthought, she donned a pair of hot pink flip-flops. If she was going to act like a tourist, she might just as well look like one.

When Katherine caught sight of Angela's getup, she started laughing. "Well, at least you won't be alone. Flip-flops and zinc oxide are the dress code down here. I hear even the dolphins wear them once in a while."

"Hardee, har, har." Angela playfully pushed Katherine out the door.

Down on the street, things were already in high gear. It seemed as if every tourist on the island was present to take part in the activities. Several applauded as an acrobat tiptoed across a tightrope strung between two lampposts while others cringed as an escape artist tried to free himself from a straightjacket wrapped in chains. Mimes passed themselves off as marble statues; jugglers lobbed swords, torches, and barbells high into the air; scantily garbed beauties performed pirouettes on unicycles. Artists displayed their masterpieces; hawkers pitched gaudy sun-visors and tee shirts; and crowds fought to get close to the food carts that cluttered the narrow streets. One vendor sold funnel cakes, another shrimp kabobs. There were smoothies, lemonade, popcorn, and key lime pies, cookies, and brownies.

It had been more than five hours since their seaside lunch and Angela could feel her stomach rumbling as Katherine pushed her toward a waterfront patio. "This place will be packed in a few minutes. Let's grab a table before they're all gone."

"Is this Sloppy Joe's?"

"No, but it's not far from here. We'll have a drink or two and watch the sunset then we'll go get some dinner."

"I'm not so sure that drinking is such a good idea. My hands were starting to itch so I took an antihistamine before we left and now I'm feeling kind of drowsy." She rubbed some of the zinc oxide from her nose onto her hands. Maybe that would help.

"Well if you're worried about mixing drugs and booze just order a Shirley Temple or an iced tea. You've got to have something to toast the sunset with."

Toast the sunset? Why? Was it going somewhere?

By the time the drinks arrived, all the tables were filled up. The sun hung low in the sky sending shafts of light slicing through cotton candy clouds and melting into the darkened water. At first, Angela could make out people's features but as the sun dropped closer to the endless horizon and the sky morphed into thick layers of indigo, burgundy, and burnished gold, all she saw were faceless silhouettes.

When the sun finally merged with the water, everyone, including Angela, raised their glass and cheered. "Now I can see what all the fuss was about. I don't think I've ever seen anything so beautiful."

"Honey, like they say, you ain't seen nuttin' yet. Let's get some dinner."

Grabbing her arm, Katherine dragged Angela through the crowd, down the cobbled street, and toward a one-story building that took up the better portion of the block and both sides of one corner. The sounds of people having too good of a time radiated out of jalousied windows and a sign on one of the doors boasted that the place opened at nine in the morning.

"Is THAT where we're going?" To Angela,

the place looked like a dump.

"Why not?" Katherine seemed surprised that Angela would ask such a question.

"Well, for starters there's a big black guy blocking our way."

Sure enough, a huge cocoa-skinned male with dreadlocks, an embroidered vest, and a crocheted skullcap stood in the doorway. A long scar starting in the middle of his forehead descended past his right eye and curved down across his cheek until it met up with the edge of his lip.

"Don't worry. I know him."

Katherine pulled Angela closer to the door and extended her hand toward the man. "Wh'appen, idren?" They exchanged a friendly though mysterious-looking hand-shake.

"Well kiss me neck gai. Yuh noh dead yet?" The man grinned and revealed several gold teeth. "Wanna nice up wid sum natty con-gos?"

Katherine let loose of the man's hand and pretended to look offended. "Don be no boda, breeda. Yuh looks kinda winjy to me. Tinks we'll jus jook an jam a bit."

"Sure nuf," The man stepped aside and motioned for them to enter.

"What was that all about?" Angela had heard about Rastafarians but she'd never met any. At least, not until then. Meeting this one frightened her enough that she considered foregoing dinner so she could race back to the condo and hide.

"Oh, the big guy with the dreads asked if we wanted to party and I told him that we were just gonna hang out and get some food."

"Was he trying to pick you up?"

"Sure. But I told him he's not my type."

Angela wasn't quite sure what that meant because as far as she could tell there wasn't a man alive that wasn't Katherine's type.

As the women walked into the bar, the big Rasta yelled out, "Mi link yu up layta, biscuit."

"Not if I can help it," hissed Katherine.

The inside of the bar was almost as gnarly as the outside. White-bearded Hemingway look-alikes stood three deep at the bar, most of them with their fists wrapped around beer bottles and their arms around bikini-clad women. From a back room, the sounds of cheers and jeers indicated there was probably a lot of gambling going on. Up on a stage, musicians pounded out a rhythm on aluminum washboards and tambourines. The effect was deafening.

"This place has been around since 1937," yelled Katherine. "It used to be called the

Silver Slipper but when Hemingway told Joe Russell that his bar looked like a pig pen, the name got changed to 'Sloppy Joe's.' "

"Appropriate name." Angela fought to keep her shoes from sticking to the floor. If this was the hottest place in town, she wondered what the rest were like. As far as she could tell, Sloppy Joe's was nothing but a trashy bar where gambling, drunkenness, and promiscuity were acceptable behavior. Somehow, Katherine fit right in.

"You should see this place on New Year's Eve," shouted Katherine as she maneuvered her way across the dance floor toward an empty table. "Instead of dropping a ball like they do on Times Square, they drop a conch shell. It's really cool. If you don't get any better offers, you ought to come down here with Mongo and me."

"Better offers? From who?" Angela wiped stray crumbs from a chair and sat down at the table. When she laid her arm on the table, she discovered it was as sticky as the floor.

"Oh. I don't know. Like maybe Gil Fontero?"

"Get real, Katherine. He's too old for me. Besides, from what I hear he's got his pick of women. Why would he ask me out for

New Year's Eve?"

"Because he likes you."

"What makes you think that?"

"It's the way he looks at you. Kind of hungry if you know what I mean."

"Yeah, well I'm plenty hungry right now. How about we order?"

"You got it, girlfriend." Katherine waved one of the waiters over to the table and ordered "a couple of Rum Runners and two jerk sandwiches on Cuban bread."

"What the heck is a jerk sandwich?" Angela's hunger was making her irritable.

"Don't worry — it's just a spicy chicken sandwich."

"Good thing. You had me worried for a minute. This place makes me nervous. Is it safe to eat here?"

"Listen, Angela," Katherine leaned across the table so she wouldn't have to scream. "I know a lot of people don't approve of me but believe me when I say I won't let anything bad happen to you. I sort of feel like you're my kid sister."

"Thanks for that, Katherine. It's just that I'm not used to places like this."

"I know. Tony said you led a sheltered life."

"Sheltered? What does he know about sheltered? He's always been free to do and go wherever he pleased. He left home and joined the army when he was barely eighteen and he got married when he was twenty. I never got to do half the stuff he did. I always had to behave because I was a girl. I just wish he'd mind his own business and stay out of mine."

The waiter placed two drinks on the table and Angela downed hers in one gulp. "Waiter? Bring two more of these and keep 'em coming." So much for not drinking.

"Hey, Angela, take it easy. There's three kinds of booze in that drink. I'll be picking you up off the floor before the food even gets here."

"Who cares?" Angela sucked on the melting ice.

Four drinks, two jerked sandwiches, and half a key lime pie later, Katherine and Angela left the bar. On their way out the door, the Rastafarian bid them, "More time, gais."

"Yeh, mon." Angela blew her new best friend a kiss and stumbled down the street.

The next morning, she awoke with a throbbing headache and a bandage wrapped around her ankle. Pulling the bandage aside, she discovered a very large, very colorful butterfly gracing her once-unblemished leg.

"Oh, my gosh. What have I done? Tony is gonna have a fit."

8
THANKSGIVING

When Katherine pulled up in front of the whitewashed block building that housed the Cay Turtle Hospital, she jabbered something about, "the word C-A-Y, pronounced Key," coming from a Spanish word meaning small, low island made up of sand or coral. Angela could have cared less. All she could think about was getting inside the hospital. From what she'd heard, sea turtles were on the endangered species list and this might be the only chance she'd get to see one even if it wasn't in the wild.

Inside the hospital, a woman wearing a Chicago Cubs baseball cap sat behind a scruffy-looking banquet-style folding table. Angela guessed the woman was probably in her thirties or forties but it was hard to tell anymore because everyone under forty looked like a kid to her. There was a rotary-dial telephone on one corner of the table and a very large, very black Underwood typewriter smack dab in the middle. Apparently, the hospital operated on a not-so-generous budget.

The baseball-capped woman had been reading a paperback novel but quickly set it aside when Angela and Katherine entered. "Good morning, ladies. Welcome to Cay Turtle Hospital. Are you here for the ten o'clock tour?"

"No," replied Katherine. "We were just passing through and thought we'd drop in and see what was going on."

"Oh, I'm sorry. But tours are by reservation only. The next one starts at one o'clock. Would you like me to put your names on the list?"

A man dressed in green scrubs stepped out of an adjoining room. "You'll do no such thing, Jillian. These ladies are friends of mine. I'll show them around myself." The man was Gilberto.

"Hey Gil," squealed Katherine. "What are you doing here?"

"I'm a volunteer. I help with whatever needs to be done. They brought two injured turtles in last night and I was just out back getting them ready for surgery."

"Surgery? I thought you were a cook." Angela gave Gilberto a thorough once over. Somehow, the scrubs made him look slimmer and younger. Maybe that was how he attracted so many women.

"Oh," laughed Gilberto, "I don't do the surgery. I just help get the turtles ready for the doctors."

"So, what happened to the big guys?" asked Katherine.

"They got tangled up in an abandoned fishing net but, luckily, some divers spotted them and notified us before the turtles drowned. One of them has a broken flipper, the other one has a cracked shell."

"Will they die?" Tears rimmed Angela's eyes.

"Not if we can help it." He seemed concerned about the turtles' well-being. Maybe he wasn't such a sleaze-ball after all.

"Come on, I'll show you around."

Gilberto led the way down a short corridor and through a set of swinging doors. Out in an open area several tanks and pools were filled with turtles of various shapes and colors.

"This is our rehabilitation center," he said. "We bring the turtles here after surgery so that we can give them medicine and watch their progress. Once they're well enough, they get released back into the ocean. Those that can't be released live out their lives in the big pool out back. Come, I want you to meet someone."

Angela and Katherine followed as Gilberto led them to a salt-water pool surrounded by a chain-link fence and covered with a shade-cloth-canopy.

"See that reddish-brown turtle swimming along the far side?"

Angela and Katherine leaned against the wire fence and strained to look into the murky water.

"You mean the one with the big head?" asked Angela.

"Yes. He is a sixty-year-old, three hundred pound loggerhead. I call him Ol' Yeller because his plastron is yellow."

"Plastron?" Gilberto seemed well-versed in more than just cooking terms.

"I'm sorry. His underside. If he turns over, you'll see it."

"So, what happened to him?" Katherine sidled up to Gilberto and put her arm around his waist.

"He had fibropapilloma tumors all over his neck and mouth. That is a type of viral tumor that affects more than 50% of the sea turtles in the Keys. The doctors were able to remove the tumors before they infected his internal organs but not before they got into his eyes so although the tumors are gone, he is blind and will have to stay in this pool for the rest of his life."

"That's so sad," sighed Angela.

"Not really. We feed him well, make sure he gets plenty of exercise, and he's always got three or four lady loggerheads to keep him company."

"The lucky cuss," crooned Katherine. "Sort of like you, huh Gilberto?"

Gilberto didn't dignify Katherine's question with an answer. "Want to see the nursery?"

"You've got babies here?" Angela couldn't believe her luck. Not only had she seen an adult sea turtle for the first time in her life, she was going to get to see babies as well. This final stop before heading home was turning out to be the best part of the trip. Her hands and lips had even stopped itching.

"Unfortunately, yes. People find eggs and hatchlings on the beach and either take them home or bring them here. Of course, it is illegal to handle or transport turtles unless you have the proper permit, but a lot of people do not know that."

Or they just don't care, thought Angela.

Gilberto walked toward two aquariums. "The tank on the left has turtle eggs buried in the sand and the one on the right has baby turtles that hatched within the last couple of days."

"How long does it take for the eggs to hatch?" Angela was fascinated.

"Sometimes as long as sixty days, sometimes as short as a week."

"Then what?" she asked.

"We keep the hatchlings in the seawater tank for a week or two and when they get to be about two inches long we release them into the ocean."

"Do you keep any for soup?" quipped Katherine.

"No, Katherine. We do not."

"What a pity. I hear turtle soup is delicious."

Angela grabbed Katherine by the elbow and started pulling her away. "Come on, Katherine. I think it's time we headed home and let Gilberto get back to work."

"Oh, yeah. Well, thanks for the tour, Gil. Will we see you later?" Katherine didn't seem ready to leave.

"Probably not tonight but I am sure we will run into each other sometime soon."

"Hope so." Katherine waved over her head as Angela pushed her out the door.

The next couple of weeks flew by quickly for Angela. Her hornet bites healed, she went back to work, and before she knew it, Thanksgiving had rolled around. Since

Angela's trailer was so small, Fran suggested having Thanksgiving dinner at her house. That suited Angela just fine because, although she could whip up a pretty decent tuna salad or spaghetti sauce, she preferred leaving holiday meals to someone else. That way the only thing she had to worry about was what to put in her mouth.

Up until that point, Angela had worn socks and long pants so that Tony wouldn't notice her tattoo. She wasn't afraid of him, she just didn't want him losing his temper before she was ready to deal with it. Knowing she would have to let him see it sooner or later, she decided Thanksgiving dinner would be the perfect time. Fran said some of her relatives and a couple of neighbors would be there. Tony wouldn't go off on her in front of company. Would he?

Thanksgiving morning was a scorcher. Even before the Macy's parade began, the temperature had reached eighty degrees. Angela looked through her closet and spotted the green dress. No telling how long the warm weather would last. She might as well get her money's worth and wear the dress again. She'd even put on a pair of heels. They'd show off her shapely legs and new tattoo. That should make her the talk of the party.

Tony was sitting on the patio when Angela arrived at his trailer. It was only noon but four empty beer cans already sat in front of him.

"Getting an early start?" jibbed Angela.

"Yeah. We're gonna have a full house today and I'm preparing myself. Want one?" Tony pushed an unopened can toward his sister.

"No thanks. I'm trying to cut back. Besides, I've got to save room for all that delicious food Fran's cooking."

"Don't kid yourself. Most of it comes from the Publix deli. Fran takes the easy way out of everything."

"Wow. That's a little harsh, isn't it?"

"Just telling it like it is. Got a problem with that?"

"No . . ." Tony seemed a little out of sorts so Angela decided to leave him alone.

"I think I'll just go inside and check things out."

Fran seemed to have everything under control. Serving dishes, plates, napkins, and flatware were set out on the side-board, most of the living room furniture had been pushed aside and replaced with linen-draped card tables and folding chairs, three pots were boiling away on the stove, and from the smell of it, the turkey was well on

121

its way to becoming dinner.

"Well, don't you look nice? Did I forget to mention that today was going to be casual?" Fran wore a grease-stained dishtowel tucked into the waistband of her denim shorts.

"You told me but I wear grubbies all week so I thought it might feel good to get dressed up for once. Too much?"

"No, but I'd get rid of the shoes . . . wow . . . is that a real tattoo?" Fran spotted Angela's tattoo. From the smirk on her face, it appeared she approved.

"Like it?" Angela twisted her ankle so that Fran could get a better look.

"It's wonderful. When did you get it?"

"When Katherine and I went down to the Keys a couple of weeks ago."

Fran inched closer to Angela and whispered, "Has Tony seen it yet?"

"No. Why?"

"I wanted to get one once and he threatened to leave me. Said if God wanted women to have tattoos they would have been born with them."

"Oh, but he thinks it's okay for guys to have them?"

"You know your brother."

"Yeah. I do."

An hour later, the trailer was filled with friends, relatives, and neighbors, most of whom Angela had never met. They'd all introduced themselves but Angela couldn't remember half of their names. She was never very good at that sort of thing.

Around the time Fran set the food out and everyone started to fill their plates, Tony finished off his first six-pack and came in for replenishments. Angela thought his color was a little off but she didn't say anything. Maybe he was just tired. When he took a seat at one of the empty card tables and buried his head in his hands, she began to worry.

"Are you alright, Tony?" she asked.

"Yeah. Too much sun. Could you get me a glass of water?"

As Angela filled a glass with cold water from the refrigerator, she motioned for Fran to come over.

"Whatcha need?" asked Fran.

"Nothing," replied Angela. "Tony's acting a little strange."

"How so?" asked Fran.

"He came in, sat down, and asked me to get him a drink of water."

"Water?"

"Yeah. Look at him over there." As Angela said the words, her brother slipped from his chair and landed on the floor.

"Quick," yelled Fran. "Call 911."

Within minutes, the paramedics pulled up in front of the trailer and hurried inside.

"Everyone but family is gonna have to leave," one of them ordered.

Angela ushered everyone outside, assured them that Tony would be okay, and apologized for having to rush them off before they'd finished dinner. "Maybe you can come back for leftovers tomorrow." She tried to act nonchalant but the quiver in her voice gave her away.

Everyone told Angela not to worry but how could she not? She'd planned on confronting her brother with her new tattoo — her symbol of independence — and now he was lying on the floor of his trailer with two paramedics and one surprisingly composed wife hovering over him. What if he died? That reality was more than she could handle. She crumpled into the chair Tony had been sitting in earlier and started to cry. Just then, a hand touched her shoulder.

"Don't worry, Angela, Tony will be fine." Gilberto sat down on one of the patio chairs and took Angela's hand in his. "He has had these episodes before."

"Gilberto. What are you doing here? You weren't at the party, were you?"

"I was on my way back from the shelter when I saw the ambulance pull in."

"The shelter?"

"Yes. The homeless shelter. I helped serve Thanksgiving dinner."

"First turtles, now homeless people. What are you? Some kind of humanitarian?"

"No. I just like to help out whenever I can."

"What did you mean about Tony having episodes like this before? Is he sick?"

"He's been having some heart problems. Was he drinking today?"

"Yes. He'd almost finished a six pack when I got here."

"That's bad. The doctors warned him to take it easy. Do you know if anything was bothering him today?"

"Nothing I can think of." Before she could say anything else, the paramedics wheeled Tony out of the trailer and into the ambulance.

As Fran climbed in beside her husband she told Angela that Tony was stabilized but would have to stay in the hospital for a day or two. "Nothing to worry about but if you want to come see him later, I'm sure he'd appreciate it. Gil can drive you. Right Gil?"

"Of course, Fran. Stay with Tony. Angela and I will see you later."

Several hours later, after assuring Gilberto, Katherine, and everyone else that she'd be alright, Angela changed from the green dress into jeans and a t-shirt and drove herself to the hospital.

Hospitals were not one of Angela's favorite places. They were where her mother spent a lot of time when she was a child, where her father died when she was a teenager, and where her aunts and uncles had things cut out or put in. They reeked of death and illness, their hallways were usually painted pea soup green, their parking lots were always full, and they served tasteless food and stale coffee. Hospitals were cold, impersonal places where people went to die. Whenever possible, she stayed away from them. Yet within the last two months, this was her second time in one.

Tony's room was on the third floor. Unlike the room she'd been in after her hornet encounter, this one looked like it had been professionally decorated. The walls were the color of an early morning sky, several framed prints showed sailboats skimming through the serene waters around some unidentified island, and a large picture window draped in paisley chintz looked out, not across rooftops, but upon a white sand beach and the ocean beyond. There were two beds in the room but only one was occupied.

"Who'd you have to bribe to get this room?" joked Angela as she set a vase of flowers on the food tray.

"It's one of the perks for being a frequent visitor," he replied.

"Yeah? So how many times have you been here?" She pulled up a chair and sat down but noticed it was so low that Tony had to strain to look down at her. "Think anyone would mind if I sat on the windowsill?"

"Go ahead, it looks like it'll hold ya."

Angela jumped up on the windowsill, making sure she crossed her legs so that Tony wouldn't see the tattoo. "So what's the deal? Why are you here, Tony?"

"It was just a fainting spell. I've been getting a lot of them lately."

"Really? Why?"

"Oh, I don't know. Something about my blood sugar being too low. The doc says I'm supposed to eat breakfast and then have a bunch of small meals throughout the day but how can I do that when I'm always working?"

"You weren't working this morning."

"You're beginning to sound like Fran."

"And what's so bad about that?" asked Fran as she walked into the room. "Someone's got to pound some sense into you."

"Gimme a break, Fran. Can't you see I'm

flat on my back?"

"Better on your back than in your grave."

"In his grave? He said it was just a fainting spell." Angela was beginning to feel like she could faint.

"I'll bet he also told you he had low blood sugar. Right?"

"Fran, that's enough. Angela didn't come here to listen to us bicker."

"If you don't tell her, I will."

"Tell me what?"

"Thanks a lot, Fran." Tony shot his wife a "we'll talk later" look. "Okay, so I had a heart attack last year and the doctor said I had to lose weight and stop drinking or I'd have another one."

"Why didn't you tell me? I would have come out . . ."

"That's just why I didn't tell you. I didn't want you to worry."

"Well, I'm worried now so what difference does it make if it was then or now?"

"I know. I know. I figured I could handle things myself but then I started having fainting spells and when you told me what was going on with your job I thought you could help."

"How?"

"By learning the business and eventually taking over."

"Me?" He had to be kidding.

"Sure. Why not? Fran and I talked about it and decided it would be a win-win situation. You'd have a job and place to live and I'd have someone to run the business."

She should have known. Tony hadn't offered her a job out of the goodness of his heart — he wanted something from her. It was just like when they were kids. Whenever he didn't want to do something, he got her to do it. Of course, he always made it look like he was doing her a favor. Like now. Nothing had changed — Tony was still using her.

"Gee, Tony. I don't know. This is all so sudden." As Angela jumped down from the windowsill, her jeans leg rode up.

"What the heck is that?" Tony pointed toward Angela's ankle.

"Oh. Yeah. I've been meaning to tell you about that." Angela tried to smooth her pants into place but it was already too late. Her secret was out.

"What are you trying to do? Give me another heart attack?"

Angela's head was spinning. She wanted to tell Tony that she didn't want to run his business and that all she wanted to do was be on her own, away from him and his manipulations. But how could she say something like that when he was sick and desperately needed her help?

9
GAME TIME

The doctors told Tony he hadn't had a heart attack but if he kept going the way he was, there was no question he'd soon have one. That meant plenty of rest, healthy food, lots of fresh air and exercise, and no drinking. But Tony had no intention of doing what the doctors told him. Why should he? As far as he was concerned, he'd already seen all there was to see and done all there was to do. He'd just as soon sit back and let the world pass him by.

It didn't take Angela long to figure out that if she didn't go out on service calls, no one else would. If the service calls didn't get made, people would find another exterminating company and Tony would be out of business. If that happened, she'd be out of a job again. Only this time, no one would come to her rescue.

Early one morning while she was driving to her first appointment, Angela got a call from Tony. He said Steve and Monica had noticed termites around their trailer and that she should stop by their place before she finished up for the day. Not a problem, she thought. In fact, any opportunity to see Steve was a good one.

When Angela got to his trailer, Steve was outside on his hands and knees — very appropriate for a priest. "We weren't sure you'd be able to make it today so I went to the store and bought a can of bug spray. Think it'll work?" Steve held the can up for Angela's inspection.

Even though the label said the spray might control termites, Angela knew better. "The only thing this stuff will do is make the manufacturer rich. Check out the ingredients — the first one listed is water."

"Is that bad?" asked Steve

"Well, it's not good. Give me a minute to hook up my hoses. We'll teach those little varmints not to pick on your house."

While Angela was busy spraying the underside and skirt of the trailer, Monica brought out a jug of tea and set it on the patio table. "Would you like some sun tea, Angela?"

"Sounds great. I'm just about finished here."

The front of the trailer faced east so the

patio was out of the afternoon sun and since hurricane season was almost over, the humidity was finally dropping. Even so, the temperature soared in the mid-eighties. Tony always bragged about December being the best month of the year. If this was the best, which was the worst?

"Wow, hard to believe Christmas is just around the corner." Angela picked up her glass and took a long swig. The tea had a reddish color and woodsy aroma. Hibiscus? She'd filled up her water bottle before starting rounds that morning but that was hours ago and the bottle was long since empty. She drained the glass with her second mouthful.

"I know," replied Monica. "It's my favorite time of year." She sounded almost as bad as Tony.

When she was in Indiana, Angela began preparations for the holidays right after Halloween. She'd pull out the storage boxes, check everything over for damage, shop for whatever needed replacing, and dust off all her favorite holiday albums. By the time Thanksgiving rolled around, her Christmas shopping was done, she'd made plans on where to eat Christmas dinner, and she even knew what clothes she'd wear. But that was back in Indiana. Now that she was in

Florida, everything had changed.

"Mine too, but it's not gonna seem like Christmas without snow." Angela looked at the anemic clouds and breathed an unhappy sigh.

"Hey, that's the best part," laughed Steve. "You can get out and really enjoy yourself without having to worry about boots and gloves and mufflers."

"And I'll bet Santa wears Bermuda shorts," joked Angela.

"How'd you guess?" asked Monica.

"So how do you celebrate down here?"

"The usual ways. We put up Christmas trees and decorations, and have lots of parties and parades. You'd be amazed what a few colored lights can do." Steve's eyes sparkled as he talked about Christmas. He probably had fond memories about it. After all, wasn't Christmas one of the church's biggest holidays?

"Tell her about Winterfest, Steve."

"Winterfest?" If that was just another boozing, carousing affair, Angela wanted no part of it. She'd totally quit drinking after Tony's episode and was trying to get him and Fran to do the same.

"Oh yeah, Winterfest is really cool. It starts off before Thanksgiving with a golf tournament and ends up the week before

Christmas with a boat parade. Everyone goes all out to decorate the boats and lots of people wear costumes."

"Real boats?" Angela had a mental image of sweaty men rowing luxury yachts down concrete streets. Their muscles rippled in the afternoon sun as they pushed and pulled the heavy oars and they sang a song that sounded as if it came from the depths of the ocean. The image sent warm waves radiating through her body. Was she having a hot flash?

"Are you okay, Angela?" Monica sounded concerned.

"Oh, sure. I'm fine. I guess I'm just not used to heat this late in the year."

"Here, have some more tea." Monica refilled Angela's glass. "How are things going with your new job?"

"Okay, I guess. It's just kinda hard doing everything by myself. You know, what with Tony not being able to help."

"How's he doing? I thought the doctors said he could go back to work." Steve leaned back in his chair and balanced his glass on his knee. The hair on his legs was thick and caught Angela's immediate attention. She'd always liked hairy men. It made them seem so . . . manly.

"They did but Tony's thinking about letting me run his business."

Monica's eyebrows shot toward her hairline. "You? You don't even have a license. Do you?"

"No, but that's just a technicality. I'm just not sure I even want to do it."

"Why not? It would be a great opportunity for you," said Steve.

"I know but it's a lot of responsibility and I only planned on staying here until I got my life back together. Now that Tony is sick, everything is all haywire."

Angela knew that Tony was physically able to go back to work. It was his attitude that worried her. Ever since she arrived in Florida, he had been acting strange. He'd seemed happy to see her when she first got there but then at the party she got the feeling something had happened to change his mind. Then there was that argument. Even though they'd always had their little tiffs over the years, this one felt more serious — almost as if he was trying to get rid of her. But if that was true, why had he suddenly started to talk about her taking over the business? Was it all because of his drinking?

"So what are you going to do, Angela?"

"That's just it. I don't know. I've never had to make a decision like this before. At least, not by myself. Someone else always made decisions for me. Like my boss, my ex-husband, or my parents. But this time it just doesn't feel right. Do you know what I mean?"

"Of course we do. You probably feel like you're being manipulated and you don't like it."

Steve was beginning to sound like a preacher but Angela didn't mind. At this point, he could tell her that Tony was right and she'd probably go along with it. "I don't know if I'd use the word manipulated but, yeah, something like that."

"Give yourself some time, Angela," suggested Monica. "You know you've got a job and place to live for at least a year. Look at your options, think things over, and talk to Tony."

"Well, see, that could be a problem."

"Why?" asked Monica.

"I don't want to hurt his feelings by turning him down and who else could he get to help him?"

"He could always hire someone. There are plenty of people in south Florida looking for work." As usual, Monica was being pragmatic.

"I know. But I'm family."

"You know what? I think you need to stop worrying about work and have a little fun.

Steve and I are going to the Miami Heat basketball game Saturday night. Why don't you join us?"

"Thanks for the offer but I wouldn't want to be a third wheel."

"You wouldn't," replied Steve. "Gil usually goes with us. We could double date."

Double date? The man was practically old enough to be her father and she wasn't even sure she liked him. Her life was complicated enough already. Why should she get mixed up with some guy that was probably out for no good? "Oh, I don't think so . . ."

Monica leaned forward on the small table. "You said other people were always making decisions for you, right? How about this? You're going."

That was it. The decision had been made. Now instead of just agonizing over Tony and his business, Angela also had to worry about spending an evening with the notorious Mr. Fontero. What would she do if he made a pass or tried to kiss her? Should she let him? Just the thought gave her the jitters.

By the time Saturday rolled around, Angela was a basket case. She'd messed up two appointments and ended up spraying one house for spiders and another for grub worms when it was supposed to be the other way around. If she was lucky, the homeowners wouldn't notice. If she wasn't so lucky, Tony might end up with a lawsuit. She didn't want to admit that the mistake was caused by her lack of concentration but what else could she blame it on? Chemical fumes? No. Tony had been in the business too long to accept that. If anyone complained, she'd just accept responsibility and offer her resignation. Maybe that would solve all her problems.

The Heat played at the American Airlines Arena about an hour's drive from Egret Cove. Since Monica and Steve occupied the front seat of their crew cab, Angela and Gilberto sat in the back. Angela thought it was a little too close for comfort but what else could she do? Ride in the bed?

After walking half-a-mile through the parking structure, Angela looked around at the arena. "Wow, this place is gigantic."

"Haven't you ever been to an NBA arena?" asked Monica.

"No. The only basketball games I've ever been to were at the Kokomo High School Gym." Why did she have to say that? It made her sound like such a bumpkin.

Steve and Gil bought enough nachos and sodas to last through two games then led the girls into the playing area. Large television screens were hung around the perimeter of the court but their center court seats were close enough to the action they would be able to see the point guard's smile if they wanted to.

The game moved fast. By the end of the first quarter the Heat were beating the Golden State Warriors and the crowd was going wild. In the second quarter, one of the umpires called a personal foul against a Miami player who came into illegal contact with one of the Warriors. The Warrior got two free throws, sunk them both, and put his team ahead. Angela stood up and began to boo but Monica quickly pulled her back into her seat. "Calm down, Angela. There's still the second half."

During halftime, a group of twenty mature women carrying pom-poms and wearing gold mini-skirts paraded into the center of the arena. A hidden announcer boldly proclaimed, "Ladies and Gentlemen. Let's give a warm welcome to Miami Heat's famous Golden Oldies Cheerleaders."

The crowd hooted and hollered as the geriatric matrons gyrated across the floor, shaking their hips, kicking their feet into the air, and doing somersaults all in perfect rhythm to Roy Orbison's *Pretty Woman.*

"Hey. I've heard about them," laughed Angela. "Katherine said she tried out with them once but didn't qualify because they said she was too sexy."

"Yeah, right. It's more likely they thought she was an exhibitionist," sneered Monica

"I am sure you could get in if you tried," volunteered Gilberto.

"Oh, no. I could never do anything like that. I'm too old." Angela could feel her face going red.

"What do you mean too old?" asked Steve. "Some of those women are twenty years older than you. If they can do it, so can you. After all, you don't quit playing when you grow old, you grow old when you quit playing."

What was going on? Tony had said practically the same thing the night of the party. Now Steve? Did everyone think she was acting like an old crone? Were they right? And, if so, was there anything she could do about it?

Not that it made any difference to Angela, the Heat ended up beating the Warriors 102 to 93. It had been a confusing evening for her and all she wanted to do was go home and think. On the way back to the trailer park Gilberto asked when she was going to try out for the Golden Oldies. Her reply was an emphatic "Never."

But the thought stayed with her. Even

after arriving home and getting ready for bed, she kept thinking about it. "Why not?" she asked Gizmo. "I'm in fairly good shape, I like oldies music, and I could probably fit into one of those gaudy uniforms."

The dog just stared at her.

"Oh, I know what you're thinking, boy. 'You left me alone all night and now you're talking like a crazy woman.' Am I right or what?"

Gizmo jumped up on the bed, laid his head on a pillow, and went to sleep. Angela pushed him over and curled up beside him. She'd wanted to spend some time thinking about what to do with the rest of her life but as she unconsciously stroked Gizmo's head, she drifted off to sleep and fell into another dimension.

She saw herself moving across the floor to music being played by Steve, Monica, Fran, and Mongo who, instead of playing an oldies tune, were doing their rendition of *The Dance of the Sugar Plum Fairies.* Her hair was shorter and surprisingly blonde — almost the same color as the eye-catching lamé sarong she wore. And she had tattoos all over her body.

Katherine yelled, "You go girl," while Gilberto lavishly threw kisses and Tony shook his head sadly and grumbled, "Shameful.

Shameful."

She felt young and free and full of life. But somewhere in the back of her mind, she knew it was only a dream.

10
SOUTH BEACH

While everyone in the Midwest was digging out from under eight inches of new snow, Angela was having the time of her life. She checked out the boats at the Winterfest celebration. She ate *pastalitos* and drank *café cubano* in Little Havana. She cheered Santa as he surfed off one of Miami's white sand beaches. She danced to reggae music at the King Mango Strut in Coconut Grove. In honor of the season, she even bought a three-foot-tall Christmas tree, decorated it with seashells and glittery mermaid ornaments, and exchanged gifts with all her new friends. Maybe Florida wasn't so bad after all.

Needless to say, by the time New Year's rolled around, she was so partied out that she turned down Katherine and Mongo's invitation to ring in the new year with them at Sloppy Joe's. Staying home and watching Dick Clark was about the only thing she had enough energy for. Nonetheless, when Katherine mentioned that her Foxy Ladies group was planning to spend a day at South Beach, Angela jumped at the chance. She'd heard a lot about the legendary beach and wondered if it was half as tawdry as everyone said it was. Katherine would be the perfect tour guide.

The outing was scheduled for the last Monday in January, which, according to Katherine, would be ideal because, "most of the pool boys have that day off." Afraid to ask what that meant, Angela just nodded and whispered, "sounds like fun."

Taking a weekday off meant Angela had to reschedule all her appointments. Even though all the snowbirds were manic about bugs, once she told them she'd give them an extra discount, they all agreed to the change. The only appointment Angela didn't change was with Gramma Snodgrass, the chain-smoking old woman who was obsessed with aliens.

Shortly after Tony's Thanksgiving Day scare, the eccentric old woman began complaining more and more about little green men getting into her trailer. They crawled in under the doors, squeezed in through the windows, and slithered down the air vents. They shot laser beams on her from their spaceships, they followed her every move, and they injected toxic drugs into her system. Even though Angela knew the "little green men" were nothing but insects looking for a winter home, she stepped up her visits from twice a month to once a week. Tony said she was wasting her time with the peculiar woman but as far as Angela was concerned, Gramma Snodgrass was harmless and the weekly visits seemed to comfort her. Sometimes it just felt right to do something nice.

Angela usually swung by Gramma's place at ten in the morning but since Katherine wanted to be on the road by then, she moved the appointment up to eight. With any luck, the old woman would be awake and at least somewhat coherent.

When Angela pulled up to Gramma's trailer, she had to park in the street because a big Chevy Suburban was parked in Gramma's junk-filled carport. "Humph. Looks like Gilberto's truck. Wonder what he's doing here."

Before Angela could pull on her white coveralls, she found out.

"*Ciao,* neighbor." Gilberto stood in the doorway with one arm arrogantly wrapped around the old woman's shoulders. "You are out early this morning."

From all appearances, Gramma Snodgrass and Gilberto Fontero knew each other pretty well. In fact, judging from the old woman's lop-sided grin, it appeared they were a lot more than friends.

"Can't be," she mumbled.

Gilberto cupped a hand to his ear and shouted, "What did you say, Angela?"

Angela shouted back that she had moved Gramma's appointment up because she was going to South Beach for the day.

"What is in South Beach?" he asked.

"I heard they've got a lot of Art Deco and Katherine's Foxy Ladies group was going so I decided to tag along." Angela wondered why she always felt compelled to tell this aging Casanova all the smallest details of her life. Couldn't she have just said she was going somewhere for lunch?

"That and a lot of half-naked men," tittered Gramma.

"Half-naked men?" Angela tried to act naive.

"I am sure Katherine told you," replied Gilberto. "That is the only reason she goes there."

Angela donned her best high and mighty face and stared directly into Gilberto's eyes. "Well, I don't recall her mentioning it."

"Whatever you say, Angela." Gilberto

gently maneuvered Gramma Snodgrass back into the trailer and closed the door.

"Whatever you say, Angela, whatever you say," she mimicked. "Who does he think he is? Rhett Butler?"

Angela grabbed her tank and sprayed around the perimeter of the trailer, up the steps, and under the eaves. The inside would have to wait until next week. There was no way she was going into that trailer with Gilberto Fontero inside. When she was finished, she pounded on the door and shouted, "I'm all done, Gramma. See you next week."

The only reply was a muffled, "Thank you," and then a stifled giggle.

Angela threw the spray tank into the back of the truck and wiggled out of her coveralls. "What's with that old coot?" she wondered. "He's got half the women in Egret Cove swooning over him but he still has to come over here. Isn't there any place safe from him?" She jumped into the truck, slammed it into gear, and peeled away from the trailer before Gilberto had an opportunity to come outside and ask more questions.

When she got back to her trailer, she found Katherine and four other women waiting in an eight-passenger van. Even though the windows were rolled up, Angela could hear Jerry Lee Lewis's *Great Balls of Fire* blasting from strategically located speakers. She pounded on the van door. "Hey. Turn it down before someone sends for Deputy Rambo."

Katherine rolled down the driver's side window. "Hi, Angela. We were just killing time till you got here." She was wearing a red cowboy hat trimmed with a purple feather. The combination of the hat and red hair made her look foolish.

"Where'd you get this boat?" asked Angela.

"One of Mongo's friends lets me use it whenever the group needs to go someplace. Wanna drive?"

As Katherine started to open the van door, Angela pushed it shut. "Thanks, but no thanks," she replied. "I think I'll just act like a tourist today. Give me a minute to check on the dog then we can go."

Gizmo was sleeping on the plant ledge beneath the sunroom's bay window. Even though his tail and one leg hung over the side, it was his favorite spot. When he wasn't counting sheep, he could look out the window and supervise everything that went on in the park. Even with his bad eye, he didn't miss a thing. He watched two birds build a nest in one of the hanging planters, he learned to distinguish residents from visitors, and he never missed an opportunity to bark at the neighbor's cat. After several failed attempts to convince the pampered pooch to nap elsewhere, Angela gave up, covered the ledge with an oversized beach towel, and let the dog have his way.

"Don't get up, boy," she said. "I just wanted to make sure you had enough food and water for a while."

The dog lifted his head and nonchalantly stretched his front legs — an indication he had no intention of getting off the ledge. Then he shot Angela one of those, "You're not going out again are you?" looks.

For a split second, the thought of staying home crossed Angela's mind. Then it was gone. Today was going to be a fun day and she was going to enjoy it — no matter what. Once she was convinced that Gizmo would neither starve nor die from thirst, she kissed the top of his head, grabbed her purse and sunglasses, and headed out the door.

It looked like it was going to be a beautiful day. The sky was the kind of blue Angela had never seen in smoggy Indiana. Fluffy white clouds drifted out toward the ocean, the humidity was low, and the temperature was comfortable enough that she didn't even need a sweater. She found it hard to believe it was almost February and that she'd been in Florida for more than three months. Time was flying by so fast that her year would soon be over. Then what? Stay with Tony and run his business or go somewhere else? She still wasn't sure what to do and the more she thought about it, the more confused she became. On the one hand, she felt like she had an obligation to help her brother but on the other she didn't want him calling the shots with her life. People had been doing that all of her life — her parents, her husband, that kid at the hardware store, and now Tony. It was time it stopped. Maybe she should take a lesson from Katherine and become more independent. Yeah. Right. Like that was ever going to happen.

Katherine drove the mammoth vehicle like a pro and before long they were cruising past the famous beach locals called *SoBe.* It was still early in the morning so there weren't many people on the streets.

"This is great," observed Katherine. "We'll get a good parking spot, check out the sights, and then find an outdoor restaurant where we can sit and watch the show."

"What show?" Angela knew Katherine was talking about men but she didn't want to seem too eager.

"Just wait," laughed one of the women. Evidently, she'd been there before.

After finding a parking spot, the women spent almost two hours walking through the Art Deco District pretending to be interested in the architecture, "Oh, look at those incredible eyebrow windows," commented one woman. "And just look at those colors," remarked another. They stopped at all the boutique windows and ogled the too-young, too-small fashions and wondered, "Think I'd look good in that?"

Once they reached Ocean Drive, they scoped out the restaurants and chose one with a table closest the action. It was a tight fit but all six women managed to squeeze together without blocking one another's view. They hurriedly read the menu, placed their orders, and got ready. Within minutes, the show started.

A group of well-endowed young men wearing nothing but thongs and suntan lotion roller bladed past the restaurant. Two of the women at the table whistled and the boys turned, smiled, and waved. A second group glided by, this time with several girls in tow. It was easy to tell who was with who. Boys and girls held hands. Girls and girls held hands. Boys and boys held hands. Although most of the skaters looked like they were just out to enjoy the balmy weather, others seemed more intent on putting on a show. They twisted and twirled, they rolled backwards, and two skaters did back-flips. Their barely-there, vibrantly colored string bikinis and thongs made them look like Cirque du Soleil wannabes. One of the boys suddenly tripped and fell to his hands and knees.

"Ow, I'll bet that hurts," grimaced Angela.

"Probably not as much as his thong," chuckled Katherine. "Did you sec how he grabbed at it?"

"I was trying not to look." Angela wondered if she was blushing.

"Oh come on, Angela. You know you're enjoying this as much as everyone else."

"Maybe, but I don't understand how they get away with wearing those things. Don't you think they're sort of . . . indecent?"

"No way," replied Katherine. "Mongo wears them all the time."

"Now *that's* more than I needed to know."

"Yeah? Well I'll bet you wouldn't mind seeing Gil in one."

"Gilberto Fontero? You've got to be kidding," hissed Angela.

"Hey. I've seen the way you look at him. Sort of like a little puppy and a new toy."

Katherine was obviously enjoying the banter.

"He's nothing but a dirty old man that chases around after vulnerable women."

"What are you talking about, Angela? Gil's a real sweetheart."

"Oh sure. Well, when I went to Osceola Park this morning, I caught your little sweetheart with his arms around a defenseless old lady who believes in aliens."

"You mean Gramma Snodgrass?" asked Katherine. "He goes there every Monday morning to drop off groceries. Gramma says she couldn't get along without him."

"So why did Tony tell me he comes on to all the women in Egret Cove?" Angela wondered if she should add lying to Tony's growing list of character flaws.

"I think Gil complimented Fran once or twice and Tony took it the wrong way."

"No." Angela couldn't believe what she was hearing.

"Yes. In fact, Tony got so mad he threatened to get Gil run out of the park."

"But I thought they were friends."

"Looks can be deceiving."

"Wow. And all this time I was wrong about Gilberto?"

"Well quit worrying about it and quit calling him Gilberto. He prefers Gil."

Angela turned her attention back to the skaters but, as entertaining as they were, she couldn't stop thinking about Gilberto. All this time he'd been trying to be nice to her and what did she do? She criticized him. She snubbed him. She treated him like a criminal.

Why?

11
CHANGES

"So who all's going on the swamp safari thing next month?" asked one of the women.

Angela didn't respond. Ever since leaving South Beach, she'd been so engrossed with thoughts about Gilberto that she hadn't paid attention to much of anything else. Was Gil really a nice guy or was Katherine so enamored with him that she couldn't see his faults? He'd never come on to her or attempted to lure her into a compromising situation. At least not yet. But that didn't mean it wouldn't happen. After all, he was always bringing her food and gifts. That meant he was up to something didn't it? But what if it didn't? What if he was trying to be a good neighbor? Or what if, as Tony's remarks implied, he was just waiting for his chance? Angela decided that as soon as she got home, she'd track down Gilberto Fontero and find out what made him tick.

But before doing that, she had to deal with her brother.

Tony was sitting in a plastic lawn chair in the middle of Angela's carport. Dressed in a tank top, Bermuda shorts, and flip-flops, his arms were crossed, his face was red, and he looked like he was about ready to blow a gasket.

"Where have you been all day?" he blustered. "I don't remember saying you could take the day off."

"Calm down, Tony," soothed Angela. "I rescheduled all my appointments except for Gramma Snodgrass. I took care of her this morning."

Tony's eyes narrowed when Angela mentioned Mrs. Snodgrass. "What's with you and that old woman? Getting kind of chummy, aren't you?"

"She's just lonely and needs someone to talk to. You know — you've been there."

Tony brushed back his almost imaginary hair. "Yeah, well, I think you should be a little more selective on how you choose your friends."

"What's that supposed to mean?" Angela scrunched her forehead so that her eyebrows almost came together.

"I mean running around with people like Katherine and Gilberto will get you into big

157

trouble."

"They're not so bad," protested Angela.

"Really? Katherine dyes her hair so much it's probably affected her brain. And Gilberto? Well, who knows what he's been up to."

"I thought you liked Gil."

"He's a cook," blurted Tony. "That's enough reason not to like him."

Angela shook her head and laughed. "That's silly, Tony."

"Silly? I'm just looking out for your best interests."

"Thanks but I can take care of myself."

"I'm not so sure of that." Tony squirmed out of the chair and started pacing back and forth in front of it. Angela noticed the webbing on the lawn chair left ugly red marks across the back of his legs but she thought better than to mention it. With the mood he was in, there was no way of knowing how he might react.

"What do you mean?" she asked innocently.

"I mean you need someone to take care of you. I never cared much for Carl but at least he was around when you needed him."

"Is that so? Well where was he when I broke my arm or when a tornado ripped half the roof off the garage?"

"I'm not trying to defend him or anything. It's just that I think you may have been a little hasty when you divorced him."

"He left me. Remember?" Angela thumped her chest.

"Did you ever stop to think that maybe you forced him out?"

Angela sensed her brother was up to something. He had that look that always meant he was trying to hide something. "You know what, Tony? Ever since I moved down here, you've been on my case. First you said I was acting like a prude. Then you criticized my tattoo. Now you're accusing me of running Carl off. What's with you?" Angela's temper was getting the best of her.

"Like I said, I'm just looking out for your best interests."

"Give me a break, Tony. There's more to it than that. Isn't there?"

Just then, Tony's cell phone rang. He looked at the number, mumbled, "I've got to take this," and started to walk away from his sister.

"Hey, come back here," she bellowed. "We're not finished yet."

He just waved and kept walking.

What gave Tony the right to treat her like that? She'd never done anything to hurt him. In fact, moving to Florida was as much a benefit for him as it was for her. She could have stayed in Indiana, found another house and job, and been perfectly content. But no. She pulled up stakes, drove eighteen grueling hours, and moved into a trailer. A trailer. Not even a real house. What had she been thinking?

Gizmo was waiting at the door when Angela stomped into the trailer. It didn't look like he'd been awake long. One ear was bent back and the hair along the left side of his body looked like someone had brushed it in the wrong direction. He wagged his tail and did a half-stretch, half-bow in front of his mistress.

"Well I'm glad someone is happy to see me," whined Angela. She patted the dog's head, snapped on his leash, and headed out the door. Maybe a long walk would clear her head.

While Gizmo checked out the latest bird droppings, Angela considered her situation. Every time she got around Tony, they had another argument. Nothing she did seemed to please him. She didn't use enough bug spray; she used too much. She didn't spend enough time with the clients; she spent too much. She didn't service the truck often enough; she serviced it too often. If it wasn't one thing, it was another. If she continued to let him push her around, it would get even worse. He'd tell her where she could go, who she could see, and how she should think. And there wouldn't be a thing she could do about it.

Ever since she was a kid, there had always been someone telling her what to do. First it was her parents and teachers, then her husband and that kid at the hardware store, and now Tony. No one considered her feelings. No one listened to her opinions. No one ever asked about her dreams or goals. Did they just assume she had none? All those years she just swallowed her pride and accepted it thinking that was what women were supposed to do. But enough was enough. It was time she put her foot down and stopped letting people take advantage of her. And it was time to do it now.

When she got back to the trailer, she grabbed the phone book to look up Gil's number. Upon discovering it wasn't listed, she called Katherine and asked if she knew it.

"Of course, honey," crooned Katherine. "I've got it right here in my little black book. Actually, it's a red book, but black sounds so much sexier, don't you think?"

Angela laughed and wondered if the redhead was half as cheeky as she led people to believe.

"Hurray," cheered Katherine. "Found it. Gonna invite Gil over for a quiet little tête-à-tête?"

"No," denied Angela. "I just thought it might be fun to ask some friends over for dinner. Of course, that means you and Mongo, too. But my trailer is pretty small so it'll just be the four of us. Think you can make it?"

"When is it?" asked Katherine.

"Gee. I hadn't thought that far ahead. Is Saturday night too soon?"

"It's good for us but you'd better check with Gil — you know how busy he is."

"Right. Well, give me his number and I'll find out. And unless something changes, I'll see you and Mongo at seven. Okay?

"Wouldn't miss it for the world," giggled Katherine. "What should I bring?"

"Mongo. But make him leave the sombrero home."

"You got it, girlfriend," laughed Katherine. "See you Saturday night."

A few minutes later Gilberto jumped at the chance. "Of course I'll come," he replied enthusiastically. "Can I bring something?"

"Just yourself." She hoped she wasn't making a mistake.

For the next couple of days, Angela was

so busy catching up with her appointments there wasn't much time to think about the party. When Friday afternoon rolled around and she realized she didn't have a clue about what to serve, she panicked. Knowing Katherine was probably at work, she called her sister-in-law.

"Try my favorite thing," suggested Fran. "Order a couple different entrees from the Chinese place down the street, put them in pretty serving dishes, and keep them warm in the oven until your company arrives. You can even pick up some fortune cookies and Chinese tea. Your company will think you hired a professional party planner."

"Great idea, Fran. You're a lifesaver."

"Ahh shucks. T'wern't nuttin."

It appeared that Dr. Turner had been through the same thing several times because when Angela began looking through his kitchen cabinets, she found Chinese serving dishes, chopsticks, a small assortment of colorful paper lanterns, and a menu from the restaurant Fran recommended. All she had to do was pick up the phone and place an order. It couldn't have been easier.

By Saturday evening, everything was ready when Katherine, Mongo, and Gilberto knocked on the little trailer's door. Contrary to Angela's instructions, Katherine brought dessert and Gil brought wine. "It's a Chinese rice wine," he said as he handed the bottle to Angela. "I've never tried it before but the man at the wine shop told me it was best he had. I hope it's okay."

"I really don't drink anymore," replied Angela. "But I'll put it in the refrigerator in case someone else wants to try it."

Katherine and Mongo took over the sofa, leaving the loveseat for Angela and Gil. Seeing the obvious ruse, Angela stayed in the kitchen and tried to look busy.

"You know," she said, "this is the first dinner party I've given in years. Let me know if I miss anything."

"Don't worry about a thing, honey," exclaimed Katherine. "We're all friends so just relax and enjoy."

And she did. The food was great (Mongo had seconds), the dessert was delicious, and the Chinese lanterns cast a peaceful glow throughout the tiny trailer. The wine never even got opened. As far as conversation, sex, politics, and the Foxy Ladies Society were off limits but space travel, celebrities, and reality TV were totally acceptable topics. Somehow, they seemed related.

Gizmo had been confined to the sunroom so that everyone could eat in peace but he didn't seem to mind. Once he'd greeted the guests, he jumped up on his favorite ledge and growled at a Jesus lizard that had found its way into one of the hanging baskets. When the lizard turned to stare at him, the one-eyed dog bared his teeth to reveal his unquestionable authority. Then, after determining he had adequately terrorized the despicable reptile, he victoriously crossed his front paws, laid his head down, heaved a deep sigh, and went to sleep.

Once the table was cleared and the dishes were put into the dishwasher, Angela let Gizmo out of the sunroom and curled up with him in the middle of the living room floor.

Gilberto patted the empty cushion next to him. "Why don't you come up here where it's more comfortable?"

"Thanks," replied Angela, "but Gizmo's been locked up all evening and I think he needs a little attention."

"You really love that dog, don't you?" asked Katherine.

"He's my best friend." As Angela scratched the spot between Gizmo's ears, his eyes began to close and he rolled over so that she could get his tummy.

"How old is he?" asked Gilberto.

"Going on ten. I rescued him from a shelter when he was a puppy. Some idiot shot him with a bb and he lost the sight in one eye but it never held him back. He can do things other dogs only dream about. Of course I don't let him run loose much. That would be way too dangerous."

"He's lucky to have you," said Gilberto as he sat on the floor.

Angela was afraid the Italian was about to make his move but all he did was pet the dog.

"Actually, it's the other way around," she replied uneasily. "When I first got him the people at the rescue said I'd have to spend a lot of time taking care of him because of his bad eye. But once he got used to his surroundings he sort of took over and ended up taking care of me. You should see how he acts if I stub my toe or burn myself in the kitchen. You'd think it happened to him."

Katherine and Mongo joined Angela and Gilberto on the floor. "I had a dog back in Cuba," reminisced Mongo. "She was a little Havanese with long white hair and small black nose."

"You never told me about her," grumbled Katherine. "What was her name?"

"She had one of those fancy registered names but I just called her Bianca."

"That's sweet. Could she do any tricks?"

asked Angela.

"Oh, yes," replied Mongo. "She loved to catch mice and play with them."

"Are you sure she wasn't a cat?" teased Angela.

From there on, the conversation centered around dogs. Everyone had at least one story to share. Some were funny, some were sad, and some were downright peculiar. Katherine bragged about the purebred pekinese she once owned and showed in competitions and Gilberto talked about the chihuahua one of his wives used to carry around in a leopard-skin handbag. At one point, Angela made a pot of coffee and passed around a plate of fortune cookies. When she looked at her watch, she noticed it was well past midnight. "Wow. I hadn't realized it was so late."

"Must be true what they say," chirped Katherine.

"Okay," mocked Gilberto. "What do they say, Katherine?"

"Time flies when you're having fun."

Angela smiled as her guests stretched and slowly raised themselves from the floor. There was a lot of creaking and popping but no one complained. It had been a fun evening and they all seemed to have enjoyed it. Angela wished her life could be as uncomplicated and easy-going as that evening. No arguments, no criticisms, no one telling her what to do. That's all she wanted. But real life wasn't like that and she knew it.

As they were leaving, Katherine and Mongo hugged Angela while Gilberto muttered something about having to do it again some time. Almost as an afterthought, he added, "I play bocce ball every Sunday afternoon. If you don't have anything better to do, stop by and I will give you a lesson."

"Oh, I don't know," stammered Angela. "Fran and Tony might have something planned. But I'll stop by if I can." Maybe Tony was right after all.

12
BOCCE BALLS

Angela grabbed a sweater from the hall closet, planted a kiss on the top of Gizmo's head, and rushed out the door. She'd overslept and if she didn't get moving, she was going to be late.

Ever since that prayer meeting at Steve and Monica's, Angela had been going to church every Sunday. She knew it probably wouldn't get her into heaven but it made her feel like she was paying more attention to the important things in life. Right now, that was all that seemed to matter.

When she opened her car door, she found a single yellow rose lying on the driver's seat. There was no note or anything to indicate who left it. She looked around but didn't see anyone so she placed the rose on the passenger seat, pulled out of the driveway, and sped away.

Although she should have been listening to the minister's sermon, Angela couldn't stop thinking about the rose. There were only two people who could have left it: Katherine or Gilberto. If Katherine left it, obviously, it would have been red. That left only Gilberto. But why yellow instead of red? Yellow roses meant friendship and red meant love. If the old Italian had been gutsy enough to put the rose in her car in the first place, why didn't he go all the way and proclaim his love for her as well?

Angela wondered if the rose just a nice gesture or something more sinister. She didn't like the idea of having to lock her doors and windows every night so while the minister gave his final blessing she made her mind up to confront Gilberto and set him straight on a thing or two.

Gilberto and three of his cronies were already playing when Angela arrived at the bocce ball court. It looked like the men were trying to throw large balls at a smaller ball but it was hard to tell what was really going on because they were all yelling in Italian.

"Cio illegale," bellowed one man.

"Chi dice?" snapped another.

"Compotarsi," scolded Gilberto. "Don't you see there is a lady present?"

Gilberto walked up to Angela and reached for her hand. Not sure whether he was going to kiss or shake it, she tucked her hands under her armpits and stared him down. "Don't ever try anything like that again," she hissed.

Gilberto looked confused. "Like what?" he shrugged his shoulders.

"Like sneaking around my place late at night. You're lucky Gizmo wasn't out."

"Angela, please. I don't know what you are talking about."

The confusion in Gilberto's voice and eyes caught Angela off guard. "You didn't leave the rose in my car?"

"What rose?"

"Somebody, I thought it was you, came by my trailer last night and put a yellow rose in my car. At first, it didn't bother me but the more I thought about, the more it creeped me out."

"Did you report it to security?" Gilberto looked ready to take action.

"Well, no. I was on my way to church and . . ."

Gilberto signaled to one of his friends. "Giovanni. Rush down to the gate and get Rambo."

"Why? What's the matter?" snickered the man. "Is the young lady trying to take advantage of you?"

Angela grabbed Gilberto's arm. "Please don't do that, Gil. I don't want to get anyone in trouble. Besides, it could have been Katherine or Mongo. You know how they're always doing crazy things."

"But what if it wasn't them?" pleaded Gilberto. "What if someone is stalking you?"

"Oh, don't worry about me," assured Angela. "I've got Gizmo. Remember?"

"That dog would not bite his own fleas."

"Not true," Angela exclaimed. "One time when the meter reader came into the yard, Gizmo chased him over the fence."

"Maybe so. But you can never be too careful. Have you ever thought about getting a gun?"

"Absolutely not," protested Angela. "I'd probably shoot my foot off. But you know what? It's too pretty a day to be talking about guns and stalkers. How about we change the subject?"

Obviously still concerned, Gilberto sighed and placed one arm protectively around Angela's shoulders. "Whatever you want, Angela. But first, let me introduce my friends."

Nodding his head toward the man standing closest to them and with his arm still around Angela's shoulders, Gilberto began his introductions. "This is Giovanni. He is my oldest friend and even if he will not admit it, he is older than I am. Over there," indicating toward the court, "are Vito and Aldo. In case you cannot tell, they are Irish — just like me."

Angela laughed at Gilberto's feeble attempt at humor. "Gee," she countered, "I thought you were all Texans."

With that, Vito, Aldo, and Giovanni rushed toward Angela while Gilberto hugged her closer and pretended to defend her. "Stand back," he commanded. "Touch one hair on this lady's head and you will never play bocce ball again."

The men shrank back in feigned horror. "Oh, we're sooo afraid," mocked Aldo. Then everyone, including Angela, laughed until tears rolled from their eyes.

"All right, compadres. In case you do not already know, this is Angela Dunn and she wants to learn how to play bocce ball."

"Well, I'm not really sure about that," disagreed Angela. "I don't even know what it is."

"Oh, *la bella signora*," volunteered Aldo, "I know more about this game than your pathetic friend there. Please let me explain. For beginners, calling it bocce ball is like saying Tiger Woods plays golf ball. The proper name is bocce, not bocce ball. It is an ancient game that dates back to the early Romans. Some people say it resembles bowling but, of course, it requires more skill and strategy than that boorish sport."

"Pay no attention to that pompous old fool," declared Giovanni as he pushed Aldo aside. "He's so obsessive about the game he even watches it on cable TV."

"Just that one time," protested Aldo.

"Once, smunch," scoffed Giovanni. "It's all the same."

"No it's not," defended Aldo. "That was a world class tournament."

"All right, gentlemen. Stop arguing and let's get down to business. After all, Angela didn't come here to listen to us squabble. Did you, Angela?"

"To tell the truth, it's a treat to listen to someone else argue for a change," she chuckled.

Gilberto moved back into his defensive mode. "Has someone been upsetting you, Angela?"

"Oh, it's nothing," she replied. "Just Tony trying to run my life."

"Would you like me to talk to him?"

"No. I'm sure he'll give up when he sees it isn't working."

"Well, if there's anything I can do . . ."

"Thanks, I'll be fine. Now how about explaining this game?"

"Yes. The game. Actually, it is very simple.

First, we divide into teams. Then each player rolls two large balls down the court and tries to score points by getting his balls closest to but not touching the small ball. The small ball is called a *pallino,* each frame of eight balls is called a *giro,* and a full game of bocce ball, excuse me — bocce — is called a *round.* The first team to score nine points is the winner."

"Well that's simple enough."

"There's more to it than that but we will cover the details as we move along. My friends and I will play one round and then one of them will step out and you can be on my team."

"Sounds like fun. Let's do it."

"All right, Aldo," barked Gilberto. "Since you know so much about this game, you start."

"Il mio piacere."

Aldo threw the pallino toward the far end of the court. Next, he threw one of the larger balls toward the smaller one. It landed about six inches away.

"Good shot," shouted Vito as he stepped up to the starting line. "Now, let an expert show you how it's done."

Aldo and Giovanni had joined together as one team while Gilberto and Vito made up a second. At the end of the first giro, the player whose ball was closest to the pallino was given the point. In the next giro, another man threw the pallino, and then the players threw the large balls as before. This continued until one team — Aldo and Giovanni — had accumulated nine points.

"See, I told you I was good," boasted Aldo.

Giovanni touched his thumb and middle finger together and shook them at Aldo. *"Scuzi?"* he bellowed. "What about me? I made five of those points."

"You see, Angela," chuckled Gilberto, "it is not how well you play, it's how loud you whine. Would you like to try?"

"Only if you promise not to yell if I make a mistake."

"Of course not, Angela. Of course not."

Vito moved to a bench so that Angela could play with Gilberto. Being the winners of the first round, Giovanni and Aldo threw first, then Gilberto followed. When Angela stepped up to the starting line, she accidentally placed her foot on the foul line.

"Foul," yelled Giovanni.

"Give her a break," argued Aldo. "It's her first time."

"Okay," replied Giovanni. "But next time she forfeits her turn."

As Giovanni turned his back and walked away, Angela puffed her cheeks up and wagged her head at him. When everyone laughed, she assumed an innocent face and asked, "What?"

The game progressed so rapidly that Angela didn't have time to think about the rose, her brother, or any of her other problems. All she could think about was how she and Gilberto were going to crush their opponents. Unfortunately, Aldo and Giovanni must have had the same thing on their minds because they did everything in their power to overcome Gil and Angela. They performed backhand shots, they bumped two of Gil's balls off the court, and they ended up winning the round by six points.

So as not to be considered poor losers, Gilberto offered to treat everyone to gelato.

"What's that?" asked Angela.

"You've never had gelato?" Vito made it sound like some sort of crime.

"What do I know? I'm from Indiana."

"Then you have been deprived one of the world's greatest delights," said Vito, "and we must do our best to rectify that situation as soon as possible."

"Oh, I don't know," hesitated Angela. "I should probably go home and feed the dog."

"Gizmo will be fine, Angela," assured Gilberto. "The gelato parlor is just across the road. We will not be gone long."

Gilberto held Angela's hand as they raced across the busy street in front of the trailer park. It didn't feel like he was trying to make a pass or take advantage of her. It felt right.

When they arrived at the gelato parlor, Angela was delighted. "Oh goody," she squealed. "Ice cream."

"Not just ice cream, *bambina,*" corrected Vito. "Italian ice cream."

"Do they have Rocky Road?"

"Probably not," replied Gilberto. "But they have chocolate hazelnut, mocha cappuccino, pistachio, and many different fruit flavors."

"What do you recommend?"

"Why not a little of everything?"

"Be serious, Gil."

"I am. We can get one giant sundae with all the popular flavors and share it."

"All four of us?"

"And anyone else who happens to come along." Gilberto raised his arms as if welcoming the other patrons to his feast. A couple of people smiled, others ignored him, but no one took him up on the offer.

While the young girl behind the counter was busy putting together their order, the five friends looked for a table near the window.

"The smaller the better," suggested Giovanni. "I want to get as close to that sundae as possible."

"I really had fun today," said Angela as they all sat down. "Thanks so much, you guys." She reached out and touched each of the men's hands.

"You are very welcome, Angela," replied Gilberto. "But I am still worried about that stalker."

"What stalker?" shouted Vito.

"*Silenzio,* old man," scolded Gilberto. "You will get us thrown out of here."

"*Spiacente,*" muttered Vito as he lowered his head.

Gilberto explained the situation while the other men listened. "Angela believes Katherine or Mongo may have left the rose in her car. We had dinner with them last night."

"Dinner?" questioned Aldo. "You two went on a date?"

"It wasn't a date," corrected Angela. "I just had a few friends over for dinner."

"At your house?" Aldo raised his bushy eyebrows.

"*Si,*" grumbled Gilberto. "At her house."

The discussion was interrupted when the server brought the sundae. Everyone grabbed a spoon and dug in. Then, with his mouth full of gelato, Gilberto continued. "I know Katherine and Mongo get wild some times, but this does not sound like anything they would do."

Giovanni pointed his spoon toward Gilberto. Traces of rum raisin blended with pumpkin and chocolate dripped to the table. "You know," he said as he mopped up the drops, "a couple of other women in the park have complained about similar incidents."

"Like what?" asked Gilberto.

"Mrs. Stark over on Hummingbird Lane said someone had stolen some unmentionables right off her clothesline and Betty Wilson said someone was leaving her love notes."

"That makes matters even worse," exclaimed Aldo. "Those women are so old their husbands don't even look at them anymore."

Gilberto placed his hand on Angela's. "Angela, I know you are against it but we may need to get the law involved in this."

"Not yet," defied Angela. "I want to talk to Katherine first. Now let's enjoy this wonderful ice cream before it melts."

Gilberto wasn't happy with Angela's decision but he didn't argue any further. Neither did anyone else. They all seemed to know it wouldn't do any good.

When Angela got home, she immediately called Katherine. "Did you by any chance happen to place a yellow rose in my car last night?"

"Of course not, honey," replied Katherine. "I don't give flowers to other women."

"Well, what about Mongo?"

"Nope. He's allergic to roses. One Valentine's Day he bought me two dozen red roses and his eyes welled up so bad he couldn't drive for a week. Why are you asking? Has someone been leaving you roses?"

"I'm not sure. There was one in my car this morning when I went to church. Gilberto says he didn't do it so I thought maybe it was you or Mongo."

"So . . . you went to the bocce ball court today?" pried Katherine.

"It's called bocce, not bocce ball," corrected Angela. "Yes, I went. And I ended up having ice cream with Gil and his friends afterwards. Wanna make something of it?"

"No, I think it's great. Every woman needs a good strong man to take care of her."

"Please," begged Angela. "Don't go there, Katherine. I get enough of that from my brother. I don't need to hear it from you, too."

"Sounds like I hit a sore spot."

"You did."

"Sorry. It won't happen again. Now tell me more about this rose."

"What's to tell?" asked Angela. "I got in the car and there it was. No note, no nothing."

"What do you think it means?"

"I don't know," replied Angela. "First I thought Gil was coming on to me but he looked seriously shocked when I accused him. Then I thought that maybe you or Mongo did it to say thank you for dinner. But now I'm really scared because one of Gil's friends said other women in the park have had weird things happen to them. Gil even thinks someone might be stalking me."

"Stalking is a pretty strong term. I think what we've got is a Peeping Tom. There was a story in the park newsletter about it. Seems no place is safe anymore. The park owners are even offering free self-defense classes."

"Are you going?" asked Angela.

"Yes, and I think you should go, too," replied Katherine.

"Gee. I don't know if I could hit someone."

"Get real, Angela. Every time you turn around you hear about another woman being robbed or assaulted. It's a dog-eat-dog world out there and if that means hitting some no-good thug where it hurts most, I'm all for it."

"I suppose you're right," agreed Angela. "But it just seems so cold-blooded."

"So does lying in a hospital bed."

"All right, all right. I'll go. When and where is this all gonna happen?"

"Wednesday night, seven o'clock sharp at the park clubhouse. Shall I put your name on the signup list?"

"Yeah. Whatever."

13
Do Unto Others

Despite Tony's incessant attempts to keep it from happening, Angela and Katherine were becoming best of friends. Why not? Angela needed a friend and Katherine was a likely choice. She was smart, witty, and fun to be with; she found it easy to talk to people, even strangers; she did interesting things and had been all over the world. When she wanted to do something, she never asked anyone's permission or stood around waiting for things to happen, she made them happen. She had a great sense of humor, always had a smile on her face, and never let anyone get in her way. Some people said Katherine didn't act her age, others wished they could be just like her. Sure, she was a little eccentric but it suited her. She knew who she was and she lived life to its fullest. She was everything Angela was not.

The one thing Angela didn't like about Katherine was her choice of clothes. To say her getups were peculiar would have been a glaring understatement. The truth was they were brash, gaudy, and totally age-inappropriate. Nothing, not even short shorts, mini-skirts, or thigh-high boots was off limits. But when the wacky red head showed up for the self defense class wearing red tights and a purple and pink polka-dot leotard, Angela thought she'd gone too far.

"Where'd you find that leotard?" gasped Angela.

"I made it," boasted Katherine. "Like it?"

Angela felt like running in the opposite direction but she didn't want to offend her friend so she raised her chin, threw her shoulders back, grabbed Katherine's arm, and escorted her into the clubhouse as if she were a famous beauty pageant winner.

Once inside, they discovered about a dozen women in the room. Monica and Fran, three or four women Angela had seen around the park but never spoken to, and two women who looked tough enough to take on a sumo wrestler, stood around waiting for something to happen.

Even though Gilberto suggested someone might be stalking her, Angela thought the class was a total waste of time. She knew she didn't have the nerve to hit anyone — not even a mugger. Why should she bother learning something she'd probably never use?

The instructor, a gaunt little asian who looked like he wouldn't stand a fighting chance against a three-legged chihuahua, entered the room. His over-sized *dogi* and bamboo flip-flops did little to hide his bony structure or battle-scarred toes. His voice was soft and slightly effeminate but his words captured everyone's attention. They were slow, concise, and perfectly synchronized with his militaristic movements.

"This is the twenty-first century ladies. Violent crimes are on the increase. Especially those against women."

Clutching his hands behind his back, the man continued to talk as he paced back and forth in front of the women.

"No woman deserves, causes, or asks to be attacked but it happens. In this county alone at least twenty women are assaulted every day. Many are your age. Some are younger. Age doesn't seem to matter."

He stopped pacing and placed his hands on his hips. "An attacker can gain full control in a matter of seconds. Self-defense classes will teach you how to strike first. I will teach you how to make that strike count."

Angela turned toward Katherine and

mouthed a silent, "Ouch."

The instructor scowled at her. "Ms. Dunn. Did you wish to ask something?"

"Uh . . . yeah," she stammered. "How did you know my name?"

Several women giggled but the man ignored their outburst and marched toward Angela. "The number one rule of self-defense is to be aware of your surroundings. That means knowing everything and everyone around you. Any other questions?" He scanned the room with an icy stare. When no one responded, he casually strolled toward a plump, do-it-yourself blonde wearing jute-soled espadrilles, yellow and green floral stretch pants, and a super-sized MASH t-shirt.

"Rule number two is to be prepared for the worst." The instructor grabbed the woman's arm and twisted it behind her back. When the woman attempted to scream, he placed his free hand over her mouth and in one lightning flash, forced her to her knees.

"That's how quickly it can happen," he stated arrogantly.

This time, no one giggled.

"Now, if I may have one volunteer, we will begin the class."

Katherine approached the instructor.

Locking eyes with his, she spread her feet and waited. The diminutive oriental circled her like a predator sizing up its dinner. Without anyone noticing, he placed one foot behind Katherine's and before she knew what was happening, she was flat on her back.

"You're good." Katherine moaned as she picked herself up and massaged her wounded pride.

"Yes. I know," he replied.

For the next hour, the tiny man schooled the women in the basics of self-defense. "Don't be a victim. Learn to scream. Never go out alone after dark. Always check the back seat of your car before getting in. And remember — knees and keys are your best friends." He showed them how to use their feet, elbows, and thumbs and how to kick, gouge, and maim. He gyrated his body into inconceivable positions that obviously hurt but he never flinched or backed off.

Katherine looked like she was enjoying herself but Angela wished she had stayed home. Surely, there was something a lot more interesting that she could have been doing. Like scrubbing the bathroom tile or picking lint out of the clothes dryer.

"Ms. Dunn. Is there some reason you are not taking part?" The instructor was capable of twisting his face into as many positions as his body. As he glared at Angela, one of his eyebrows shot skyward while the other aimed at his disfigured toes.

"Actually," she began, "I just came to watch. I'm not all that interested in learning martial arts."

"This is not martial arts, Ms. Dunn. This is self-defense."

"There's a difference?" Angela's sarcasm suggested she was growing tired of the man's over-inflated ego.

His voice lowered to a snarl. "If you paid attention you would see the difference."

Had she still have been in Indiana, Angela would have endured the crass remark just like all the others she'd received over the years. However, ever since moving to Florida, things had been changing. Maybe it was Katherine's influence, maybe not. Either way, instead of hanging her head and feeling ashamed, she saw red.

"How dare you talk to me like that." She poked the instructor's chest with the tips of her fingers. He responded by twirling around and kicking her arm with his foot. As the man's flip-flop went soaring off across the room, Angela screamed and pulled her wounded arm to her chest.

Katherine, Fran, and Monica rushed the

instructor and jumped him like fleas on a dog. Someone in the group yelled, "Get 'em girls" and more women joined in. All the arms and legs flailing around the room made it look like a blue light special on pantyhose at K-Mart. Within seconds, the defenseless man was buried beneath a mound of well-fed, spandex-clad, gray-haired women and one very disheveled red head.

As if on cue, Rambo burst into the room with his pistol drawn and ready. "What's going on in here?" he shrieked.

A muffled, "Help," emanated from the bottom of the heap.

"All right you women. Stand down."

The scrawny security guard started pulling intertwined bodies off the pile but by the time he reached the bottom he was so out of breath he didn't have enough energy to help the sniveling Oriental to his feet. Plopping himself on the floor, he whipped out a small notebook and addressed the instructor. "Now. Tell me exactly what happened."

Just then Mongo and Gilberto walked through the door. "Finished already?" asked Mongo as he surveyed the scene.

Seeing that Angela appeared hurt, Gilberto rushed to her side. "Are you all right, *mio amore?*" he asked.

Even though Angela felt comforted by Gilberto's concern, she tried not to react. She was beginning to like the old Italian but she wasn't ready for him to know. At least not yet. "Just get me out of here," she whispered.

While still sitting on the floor, Rambo challenged several of the women. "Why do you women need self-defense classes? You've got me."

"What about when you're not here?" one of them asked.

"I'm here twenty-four-seven. My job is to protect and serve."

"Serve yourself is more like it," mumbled Gilberto as he ushered Angela out the door.

"What's that supposed to mean?" screeched Rambo. Then as he noticed everyone was leaving, he jumped to his feet and shouted, "Hey. Come back here. I need names."

No one seemed to care.

Once outside, Angela and her friends paused to compare notes.

"Well, that was fun," chirped Katherine.

"Yeah," replied Fran. "It's a shame Tony wasn't here. He loves brawls."

"I read somewhere that most of what is taught in self-defense classes is totally useless in real-life attacks and that they just give women a false sense security," added Monica.

"Leave it to you to come up with something like that," said Katherine. "Here we are, all thinking we're doing something positive to help ourselves and you go and splash cold water in our faces."

"Maybe you should all get guns," suggested Mongo.

"Oh, sure," jeered Monica. "I can see the headlines now: *Egret Cove overrun by postmenopausal vigilantes.*"

"Ladies, please," pleaded Monica. "A little more decorum?"

"Hey. I've got an idea," shouted Katherine. "How about we all head over to my place for a little nightcap?"

"Thank you, but count me out, Katherine," replied Gilberto. "I think I will just walk Angela home. She looks a little shaken up."

"That's not necessary," objected Angela. "I can find my own way."

"I am sure you can but I would feel better if I walked you to your door. It is already dark and there might be someone hanging around in the shadows."

"Don't be silly," she scoffed.

"I am not being silly," argued Gilberto.

"Weren't you paying attention in there?"

"Watch it, Gil," warned Fran. "It's talk like that that started this whole ruckus."

Gilberto scrambled to catch up with Angela as she walked way. "I am sorry, Angela," he sighed. "I did not mean to upset you."

"You didn't," she muttered. "The truth is I'm ashamed of what I did in there and I just want to go home."

"Ashamed? From what I hear you were just defending yourself."

"I'm not sure Mr. Miyagi or whatever his name is would think so."

"It does not matter what he thinks. The important thing is you stood up for yourself. That took a lot of courage."

"It did, didn't it?" Maybe the class hadn't been a total waste after all.

The moon cast a silvery glow on the sprinkler-dampened blacktop as Angela and Gilberto walked the few short blocks toward her trailer. Except for the flicker of a few televisions, the trailers they passed were dark. Obviously, most of the snowbirds had already retired for the night. Maybe they had the right idea.

What had turned into a horrible experience seemed far removed from the peace and tranquility of the moment. It was times like this that made Angela feel like there might be better days ahead. When she turned and looked at Gilberto, she noticed his finely chiseled profile. Was he Sicilian? She couldn't remember. She'd have to ask him someday. Right now all she wanted to do was enjoy the view.

"You have changed since you first arrived here," said Gilberto.

"Really? In what way?"

"You seem more confident. More determined. I think Florida has been good for you."

"Maybe so. It's certainly been different." Different enough to turn her whole life upside down. Did Gilberto know he was part of that upset?

Gilberto gently wrapped his arm around Angela's shoulders. As they walked in silence, she wondered what life with an Italian chef would be like. Would he do all the cooking? Could he cook anything besides pasta? Would she get fat?

Winter, or what there was of it, was winding down in south Florida. Although the days were warm, the nights were still chilly so when they arrived at her trailer, Angela ducked inside, closed the windows, and grabbed a sweater. When she went back outside, she found Gilberto sitting comfortably in one of the lawn chairs.

"Well, I believe that was the last of the self-defense classes," he chuckled.

Angela pulled another lawn chair around so that it was facing Gilberto's. If there had been less light pollution, she might have been able to see the millions of stars that filled the night sky. As it was, she would settle for the twinkle in Gil's eyes.

"Probably so. Do you think we were too rough on that guy?"

"He had it coming," replied Gilberto. "He had no right to kick you. You should sue him. Maybe even the trailer park for hiring him."

"No, I couldn't do anything like that," replied Angela. "I like living here. If I sued the park, they'd probably run me out on a rail."

"Your year is nearly half over, Angela. What are you going to do when Dr. Jeff returns?"

"I don't know yet. Tony asked me to run his business but I'm not sure that's such a good idea. Isn't there some old saying about not mixing business with family?"

Gilberto pulled his chair closer to Angela's. "I think it is business and pleasure but I know what you mean. One of my nephews worked with me at the restaurant for a while. It turned into a real disaster. He was never on time, he spoiled a lot of the recipes, and he left work early whenever he had something better to do. I was the one who had to fire him and it broke my heart to do it."

"See? That's what I mean. When you work with family, something always goes wrong."

"So if you do not work with Tony, what will you do?"

"I could probably go back to the company I used to work for. They've got a store a couple miles from here."

"I thought you didn't want to work in retail anymore."

"You sure do remember things, Mr. Fontero. We talked about that the night I arrived. That was what? Four, five months ago?"

Gilberto reached over and touched Angela's hand. "It seems like only yesterday."

Angela squeezed Gilberto's fingers then quickly pulled her hand away. "Oh, there you go. You Italians are so suave."

Folding his hands in his lap, Gilberto leaned forward and stared into Angela's eyes. "I think that was also the night I promised to make osso bucco for you."

"Why, yes it was," she replied. "So . . .

when are you going to make good on that
promise?"

14
Osso Bucco

Angela sat at her dressing table sipping stale coffee, starring into the mirror, and wondering why she had agreed to have dinner with Gil. Ever since her divorce she had shied away from dating. It wasn't so much that she distrusted men, which of course was true, it was more that she was afraid of making the same mistake twice. Gil was a nice enough guy but if he was half as bad as Tony made him out to be, he could end up hurting her. She'd been through that once and once was definitely enough.

After spending most of her adult life searching for the perfect man, Angela met, fell in love with, and married Carl Singer when she was thirty-five. They bought a small farm, planted some crops and a garden, and raised a couple of goats and chickens. They were living a fairytale and, at least for a while, it looked like they would live happily ever after.

Then things began to change. Carl complained that he was working too hard for too little money and that spending long hours on the tractor was hurting his back. He said he didn't like that everything was so dependent on the weather. He even told Angela that being stuck in the boonies with her was mind-numbing and that he needed to spend more time in town. That's when he bought the store.

The store was a little hole in the wall that began life forty years earlier as a coffee and sandwich shop on the ground floor of a three-story apartment building. When the original owner decided to retire and move to the city so that she could be near her grandkids, all the equipment, appliances, pots and pans, tables and chairs, was auctioned off. The only things left behind were a long counter with six chrome and red vinyl stools that had been bolted to the floor. The store remained vacant for several years until a man from Dallas moved in, placed a couple of mail order catalogs on the counter, and brought it back to life.

Everyone in town loved that store. They could go in, sit on the polished stools, page through the catalogs, and place their orders. A week later they'd come back and pick up their goodies. The man who owned the place always kept a pot of coffee going on a hot plate and his wife brought in home baked cakes and cookies several times a week. Eventually, he even put in a couple of video games for kids to play while their mothers examined the latest sale catalogs.

The little store became a sort of community center where neighbors got together, gossiped, and exchanged recipes and farming tips. Unfortunately, when money got tight and people started coming in just for the free cakes and cookies, the man from Dallas ended up selling the business to Carl who was eager to find something that would get him away from the farm.

Carl painted the walls an anemic beige, gave the floors and windows a quick lick and a promise, and duct-taped the torn vinyl on the chrome stools. He also got rid of the coffee pot and games. He didn't want his store serving as the town's watering-hole. He wanted it to make money.

Although he knew next to nothing about running a catalog business, Carl learned quickly. He lined the walls with over-priced TVs and appliances that customers could load into their pickups and take home without having to wait a week. He made a deal with a local farmer to deliver orders to customers that didn't have pickups. He even stayed open all day on Saturdays instead of closing at noon like all the other merchants in town. Within one year, business was so good that he often spent several nights a week in town. He told Angela that staying in town gave him time to catch up on the paperwork and, for a while, she believed him.

Late one Saturday afternoon, Carl called and told Angela he was closing the store early and going to Indianapolis on business. Angela hadn't been in Indianapolis since she and Carl moved to the farm so she decided to surprise him by driving into town and joining him on his spur-of-the-moment adventure. Needless to say, she was the one who was surprised when she discovered Carl loading suitcases into an eggshell blue convertible driven by a young brunette sporting a white cowboy hat and gold hoop earrings.

Not being the type to cause trouble, Angela hid her face as the convertible raced past. Then like a wounded dog, she made her way home, devoured an entire frozen chocolate layer cake she had been saving for a special occasion, and fell asleep on the couch while *West Side Story* wound down to its disastrous, but inevitable, conclusion.

As it turned out, the dark-haired cowgirl

was just the first in a long line of women in Carl's life. Angela never talked to him about his recurring indiscretions because she thought she was probably to blame. Maybe he ran around because she had let herself go. Maybe she was spending too much time with the animals. Maybe she just wasn't interesting enough. Whatever the reason, she decided to make herself more appealing. She started wearing more makeup, bought some stylish clothes, and tried to act like a woman who didn't have to muck out goat pens or chase snakes away from chicken coops. Nothing worked.

When Carl ran off with a blonde yoga instructor, Angela felt surprisingly relieved. She finally realized she hadn't done anything wrong and that she had tried very hard to keep him happy. Evidently, he needed more. So she gave it to him: a no fault divorce that left her penniless and totally on her own. She packed up her few belongings, kissed the animals good-bye, moved back to Kokomo, rescued a dog, and made a firm commitment never to let a man hurt her again.

Angela put down the coffee cup and buried her face in her hands. Even though it had been almost fifteen years, just thinking about Carl and her ruined marriage depressed her. She felt like calling Gil to cancel their date but it was already too late. He'd probably been cooking all day. Calling him now would be cruel.

"I'll keep my distance," she told Gizmo. "We can just be friends."

The dog scratched the back of his head as if saying, "Sure, that'll work."

Shaking like a teenager getting ready for her junior prom, Angela steadied her hand as she attempted to apply eyeliner. Seeing she wasn't doing a very good job, she hastily wiped the black smudges from beneath her eyes and muttered, "I'll do without. After all, I wouldn't want to look too attractive."

By the time she arrived at Gilberto's trailer, she was so flustered that she tripped on the front steps and sent the bottle of sparkling cider she was carrying smashing into a 1957 canary yellow Thunderbird parked beneath the carport. When Gilberto rushed out to see what all the commotion was about, he found her lying spread-eagle in the middle of his patio.

"What happened?" He rushed down the stairs to help her.

"Looks like I've made a fool of myself." She brushed her slacks off and noticed a tear in one knee. "Oh, great. These are my only good dress pants."

As Gilberto helped her to her feet, Angela cried out in pain. "Ow. I think I broke my ankle."

Quickly sweeping her into his arms, Gilberto carried her into the trailer, and gently placed her on a sofa. "Let me look at that ankle," he said.

Angela didn't object as Gilberto ran his hands over and around her ankle. When he began to check her shin bone, she was thankful that she'd shaved her legs earlier in the day. But with the way her hormones were kicking in, he was probably already feeling stubble.

Without removing his hand from her ankle, Gilberto relaxed and sat on the floor. "Well I don't think anything is broken but I should probably take you to the hospital just to be sure."

"No," she objected, "that won't be necessary. Just let me rest for a while. I'm sure I'll be fine."

Gilberto helped Angela into a seated position and asked if she wanted anything for the pain.

"I brought some cider," she sighed, "but I think it went down when I did."

"Yes," he chuckled. "It looks like you have christened my T-Bird."

"I'm so sorry. I'll pay to get it washed or whatever."

"Don't worry about it. It is just a car."

"Just a car? It looks like it just came out of a showroom. How long have you had it?"

Before Gilberto could tell Angela anything about the car, his phone rang.

"Gil. Come quick." It was Katherine and she sounded desperate. "I saw a man looking in my bedroom window. He ran when I screamed but Mongo isn't home and I'm really scared. What if he comes back?"

"I am on my way, Katherine."

"What's wrong?" asked Angela.

"Katherine is in trouble. Stay here until I get back and do not let anyone in."

"No way. If you're going, I'm going."

"What about your ankle?"

"It's fine. See? I can even stand on it." Just to prove she was okay, Angela stomped her foot on the floor several times.

"If you insist. But we will take the Suburban so you will not have to walk."

When Gilberto pulled into Katherine's driveway, she came running out to meet him. "Oh, I'm so glad you're here. I was so frightened. I didn't know what to do."

"Calm down, Katherine, and tell me exactly what happened."

"Well, I saw this guy looking in my window and I screamed."

"Did he say anything or try to break in?"

Angela jumped out of the truck and rushed to console her friend. "Quit giving her the third degree, Gil. Can't you see she's upset?"

"Oh, Angela. I'm ruining your dinner, aren't I?" Katherine noticed Angela's torn pants and shrieked, "What happened to you? Has Gil been giving you another bocce ball lesson?"

"Don't worry about me, Katherine, I'll tell you all about it later. Right now, we're concerned about you. Aren't we Gil?"

Gilberto nodded and asked Katherine if she'd called Rambo.

"Yes," she replied, "but he didn't answer."

As if on cue, Katherine's phone rang. Grabbing the receiver, she was relieved to hear Rambo's voice. "Have you seen Gilberto, Katherine?"

"Why yes," she replied. "He's right here. Is anything wrong?"

"His smoke alarm has activated and his truck is gone. He needs to get back to his trailer."

"Smoke alarm? I don't understand."

"What's happening, Katherine?" asked Gil.

Katherine extended the phone toward Gilberto. "It's Rambo and he says your smoke alarm is going off."

"The osso bucco. I forgot to turn the stove off."

Angela shouted to her friend as she and Gilberto rushed back to the truck. "Tell Rambo to high-tail it over here. We've got to get back to Gil's."

Katherine snarled into the phone. "Did you hear that, Rambo? Get your skinny butt over here p-d-q."

Gilberto ran into his trailer as thick, black smoke billowed from the kitchen windows. Realizing it could be really bad, Angela bowed her head and said a silent prayer. How would she feel if something happened to him? Should she run in and try to help him?

Before she could react, a yellow and white fire engine screeched to a halt in front of Gilberto's trailer. Two men wearing yellow slickers jumped off the back end and began hauling hoses off the truck. A split second later, two axe-wielding firemen emerged from the cab and raced toward the house. Without checking to see if it was unlocked, they ripped the door open with their axes. Spotting Gilberto standing at the stove holding a smoking pot in both hands, one of the firemen yanked the pot from his hands then dragged Gilberto to safety.

Even though Angela was thankful to see that Gilberto was unharmed, she was horrified by what was happening to his trailer. The two men who dragged the fire hoses from the truck had hooked them up to a hydrant and were in the process of drenching the trailer and all its contents with water. The other two were using axes to shatter windows. Within minutes, all that was left of Gilberto's trailer was a dripping, broken mess.

"But there wasn't even a fire," pleaded Gilberto. "My home is in ruins."

"Sorry, mister," replied the fireman who seemed to be in charge. "We can't take chances with these trailers. They go up, they take the whole park with them."

A small group of neighbors had gathered to watch the firemen. "We came running when we heard the siren," said Steve. "Is there anything we can do?"

"Well, it seems I might need a place to stay for a while," replied Gilberto.

"Of course," replied Monica. "You'll stay with us as long as you have to. We've got plenty of room and we'd love to have you."

"Thank you, that is very kind. I will see if I can salvage any clothes and come over later. Right now, I have to make good on a promise and treat this young lady to dinner."

"Not after what happened," argued Angela.

"A promisc is a promise," he exclaimed. "I know a wonderful little pizza parlor in Miami. We might not get osso bucco but at least the food will be Italian."

"Are you sure? We could do it some other night."

"I insist, Angela. It will take our minds off this horrible tragedy. Besides, I am hungry. Aren't you?"

The pizza parlor turned out to be a block long affair set directly on the beach. Wrought iron tables decorated with wine bottle candles and Cinzano umbrellas dotted the sand.

"I thought you said this place was little," laughed Angela.

"I may have understated it a bit," replied Gilberto as he led her to a table and held her chair.

"Umm. This looks cozy," she said.

"Ah. Wait until you taste the pizza. It is bellisimo." Gilberto pressed his fingers to his lips and blew a kiss toward Angela.

Ignoring the gesture, she asked if she could take her shoes off. "I love the feel of sand between my toes and maybe it will help my ankle feel better. I think it's starting to swell up."

"I knew I should have taken you to the hospital."

"Don't worry about it, Gil. Let's just enjoy the view. It's so lovely, don't you think?"

Although the moon wasn't as full as it had been earlier in the week, it gave off enough light to illuminate a freighter hovering on the horizon.

"I wonder where it's going?" asked Angela.

"Actually, I think it is waiting to come in."

"Really? How can you tell?"

"Mostly from the direction it is pointed but also because it has not moved in the last five minutes."

"You're right. I hadn't notice. What do you think it's carrying? Something exotic like jewels and fine silks?"

"No, little one. More likely it is automobile parts or pvc piping."

"Oh, how exciting."

The waiter placed a large pizza, a pitcher of slushy lemonade, and two sugar-rimmed glasses on the table.

"How did he know what we wanted?" asked Angela.

"I come here often," replied Gilberto.

"They know what I like. Now — *man-giamo.*"

Whether it was the fire or the fact that she hadn't eaten all day, Angela ate more than half the pizza by herself.

"You have a healthy appetite," remarked Gilberto as he paid the check.

"You should see me with fried chicken," she replied.

"I would love to."

As they walked along the beach, Gilberto took hold of Angela's hand. "It will help steady you," he said. "Sand is sometimes hard to walk in."

Angela smiled. She knew Gilberto was probably coming on to her but she decided it didn't matter. After all, a little attention was good for a girl. An hour later when he dropped her off at her trailer and tried to kiss her good night, she acted differently. Gently pushing him away, she whispered, "Nothing is going to happen between us, Gil."

She wondered if she really meant it.

15
CRUISIN'

With Easter behind them, the snowbirds got ready to pull out of the trailer park before the summer heat and storms arrived. Lawn furniture was stowed away; golf carts were tied down; and the soon-to-be-empty trailers were sprayed for spiders, roaches, termites, or anything else that might crawl in while the fair-weather owners cooled their heels somewhere in the mountains.

Even though the exodus happened every year, it was all new to Angela. She was amazed at how quickly the park emptied out. One day all the trailers were full, the next day most of them were empty. It was almost as if someone rang a bell and everyone started running to see who could get out first. Was summer in South Florida really that bad or were people just trying to escape before the hurricanes hit? Tony had doubled up on Angela's pest-control appointments so she didn't have time to worry about what the next few months might bring. If she had even the slightest clue, she would probably have jumped ship with the rest of the deserters.

Gilberto was so wrapped up with the insurance company and trying to replace everything he lost when his trailer burned that he didn't have time for Angela. He even stopped giving her bocce ball lessons but that suited her fine because she wasn't all that sure she wanted their relationship to go any further. She kept telling herself that Gilberto was too old, too worldly, and far too flirtatious for her. Besides, she would only be in Florida for a couple more months. It just didn't make sense to start something she would never finish. Of course, Gil had the build of a thirty-year-old, spoke with the most delicious accent she had ever heard, and had a smile that made her heart pound. Every girl deserved a summer fling at least once in her lifetime. Maybe Gilberto Fontero should be hers.

Early one morning while she was leaving for her appointments, Angela noticed a silver and maroon Peterbilt hauling a new home into the park. The Oversized Load banner draped across the front of the truck was enough warning for her to keep clear. By the time she returned in the afternoon, the new trailer was set up on Gilberto's lot. As she drove by, Angela noticed Gilberto and a couple of official looking men standing outside the trailer. She waved but didn't stop. Fifteen minutes later, her phone rang.

"Angela, come see my new home." Gilberto sounded like a kid who had just unwrapped his Christmas presents. "Monica and Steve are here. We are going to grill some hot dogs and celebrate. Will you join us? Please?"

"Only if you promise not to start another fire," she laughed. Angela was surprised that she had answered so quickly. Had she unconsciously decided to take things to the next level?

"Don't even think like that," groaned Gilberto.

"I'm sorry," she muttered. "Should I bring something? Do you need paper plates or anything?"

"No, just a good appetite. Monica has prepared potato salad and some gooey-looking chocolate brownies."

"Ahh, you said the magic word," gushed Angela. "I'll be right over."

Except for plastic runners protecting the cream colored carpet and raised and secured honey-oak blinds, Gilberto's trailer was empty. "Wow. It's huge," exclaimed Angela.

"The furniture will be delivered next week," explained Gilberto. "I wanted to have enough time to prepare my new home before I started filling it with furniture."

"What's to prepare?" she asked.

"I need to get the utilities turned on, make sure the foundation is secure, wash the windows, vacuum the carpet, and of course, paint the walls."

"Paint the walls?" Angela looked confused. "They look fine the way they are."

"Yes, but they are white. I have purchased Southwestern-style furniture and the walls need to reflect the colors of the desert."

"Southwestern? I would have pegged you for Danish or Italian Provincial."

"Maybe in my younger days. But now? I want to be comfortable, not flashy. Do you know what I mean?"

"Yes, Gilberto, I do." After her divorce, Angela had moved into a small house on the outskirts of Kokomo. She decorated it in ultramodern chrome and glass furniture. It was her break from everything that screamed Carl or the farm. Within three months she realized the severity of her surroundings made her and her new dog nervous. She ran an ad in the local Penny Saver, sold everything, then went to a second-hand store and bought furniture that was beat up but comfortable.

Monica poked her head through the open door. "Hey, you two. The hot dogs are ready."

"Well, then. Shall we eat?" suggested Gilberto.

One of the few things that made it through the fire was Gilberto's picnic table. Even though it looked a little worse for wear, Monica had rejuvenated it with a lace tablecloth and silver candelabra. "I thought this was a special occasion so I pulled out all the stops. Is that okay?"

"*È bello,*" sighed Gilberto. "This is the way *al fresco* dining is meant to be."

Steve said grace, Monica passed around the potato salad, and Gilberto raised his glass in a toast. "I would like to show my appreciation to my friends for helping me through these past few weeks. Steve? Monica? You gave me a home when I had none. I know I will never be able to repay you but I would at least like to say 'Thank You' by taking you on a cruise to the Bahamas. And Angela? For being so patient while I put my life back together, I would like you to join us."

No one said a word. Monica looked at Steve. Steve looked at Gilberto. Then everyone looked at Angela.

"Gee, Gil," she stammered. "I don't know what to say."

"Say yes," shouted Monica. "It'll be fun."

"I'm sure it would be but I don't think Tony would be too happy if I missed work. We've been so busy lately he'd probably have a fit."

"We would leave on Friday and be back by Sunday afternoon," stated Gilberto. "The most you would miss would be half a day. If you wish, I will talk to Tony for you."

"No, Gil. I think I'd better talk to him myself."

As predicted, Tony hit the ceiling when he heard about the cruise. "Are you losing you mind? That old coot just wants to get you somewhere you can't escape. Do you have any idea what could happen?"

"Steve and Monica will be there and Gil said I'll have my own stateroom."

"Oh, yeah. Like one puny door is gonna slow him down."

"Quit blowing things out of proportion, Tony. Gil wouldn't hurt me."

"Really?" It was more an accusation than a question.

"Look, Tony. I'm a big girl. I've made it all these years with only a few bumps and scrapes. I can certainly make it through one lousy weekend on a boat."

"You've made up your mind, haven't you?"

"Yes. I have."

"Well don't come running to me when things turn ugly."

"Nothing's going to happen, Tony."

"I wouldn't be so sure, Little Sister. I wouldn't be so sure."

The boat turned out to be a 600-foot-long ocean liner with 300 staterooms, four dining rooms, a multi-level casino, two swimming pools, a movie theater, a duty-free gift shop, a full service spa, and two all-night disco lounges. As she was being escorted down a long corridor, Angela peeked into some of the other cabins. Most looked like standard but small hotel rooms with twin or double beds, nice carpeting, and one or two easy chairs. The outside rooms had windows, the inside rooms did not. *Not too shabby,* she thought.

When they reached the end of the corridor and the porter opened her stateroom door, Angela gasped. "Are you sure this is my room?" The porter grinned, placed her bags on a luggage carrier and asked if she was in need of anything else.

"Ah, no. Thanks so much." She handed him a five-dollar bill as he left then stood back and surveyed the room.

Off to one side, French doors led to the largest bathroom Angela had ever seen. Recessed lighting, complete with dimmer, illuminated the dressing area, sunken tub, and glass enclosed two-person shower. A large porthole window over the tub looked out over the starboard side of the ship. Or was it the port? She wasn't sure. On the other side of the room, a carved oak cabinet, probably hiding a large screen TV, was banked by two cushy-looking micro-suede sofas, a square coffee table with an exotic floral arrangement gracing the middle, and two stunning Tiffany lamps on wrought iron end tables. The main part of the cabin was taken up with a king size bed draped in an elegant white and gold comforter and a sliding glass door that led to a private veranda overlooking the prow of the ship.

Angela stepped out on the veranda and leaned against the railing. The ship was still in port so all she could see were tugboats and other vessels making their way across the channel. Once they got moving she was sure the view would change dramatically. She imagined herself sitting in the padded chaise lounge, watching massive waves cutting across the bow, joyful dolphins somersaulting along the side, and downy white clouds floating across an aquamarine sky.

What had she done to deserve this?

A soft tap at the door drew her from her reverie. Fully expecting to see Gilberto, she was almost disappointed when she opened the door and found Steve.

"Sorry to disturb you, Angela. I just wanted to let you know that Monica and I are right down the hall if you need anything. Wow. How'd you rate such a lavish room?"

"Just lucky I guess." She wondered if Gilberto was planning a late night rendezvous. "And I suppose Gilberto is close by as well?"

"No. As a matter of fact, he's on a different deck."

"Really?" Her cynicism showed.

"Yes. He said something about wanting to make sure you had privacy."

"Well, that's silly."

"That's what I told him. But you know Gil — always the gentleman."

"Right. The gentleman."

Steve ignored the sarcasm. "Anyway, there's going to be an orientation and life boat drill up on the forward deck at four o'clock. I guess we're all supposed to go. At least that's what Monica said. I wonder if the Captain knows who's really running this ship."

"Steve. Behave yourself."

"Sorry. Monica and I are going to take a walk and check things out before the orientation. Want to join us?"

"No thanks. I think I'll just get unpacked and settle in. I might even take a short nap. It's been a long day." The truth was she needed time to sort through everything that was happening.

"Well, okay. So we'll see you on deck? Four p.m. sharp?"

"You got it."

Kicking her shoes off, Angela fell into one of the sofas. Even though she had intended on thinking things over, she fell asleep. An hour later, was awakened by the sounds of shrieking bells, whistles, and horns followed by loud pounding on her door.

"Wake up, Angela. The ship is sinking."

"What? The ship? What's happening?" Angela tripped as she raced toward the door. Yanking it open she found Gilberto, Steve, and Monica standing in the hallway, holding life jackets, and laughing like crazy.

"Gotcha," shouted Monica.

"That's not funny." She looked down the hall as if trying to make sense of what was going on.

"They made me do it," laughed Gilberto as he pointed to Steve and Monica. "Steve told us you were probably taking a nap but the Captain said the life boat drill was mandatory and that everyone had to attend."

"The ship leaves in an hour. Let's get this over with," demanded Monica. "I'm in the mood for a juicy steak followed by a night of dancing."

"Dancing?" questioned Angela.

"Sure. Why not?" snapped Monica.

"Well I thought you were a . . ."

"A nun?"

"Yeah." Angela felt a blush moving up her cheeks.

"You should have seen her in the convent," laughed Steve. "Elvis would have been jealous."

After combing her hair and putting her shoes back on, Angela joined her friends as they headed for the deck where two enthusiastic crew members were demonstrating how to put on, adjust, and inflate the PFIs.

Growing up in Indiana, Angela never had the opportunity to travel on a boat. The closest she ever got was Tommy Phillip's row boat but that didn't count — it was only ten feet long. What if they hit an iceberg, she wondered. Were they even any icebergs in the Bahamas? What if she landed in the water without a life jacket? How far would she be able to swim? Did she even remember how to swim? She knew these were things she should have thought about before agreeing to come along on the trip but she was just beginning to worry about them now. She took a deep breath and bit her lower lip.

Another crew member, possibly the Captain or one of his lieutenants, pointed out where the lifeboats were located and solemnly advised everyone to "Take your time in the unlikely event something happens." Unlikely? Did that mean that something could really go wrong?

When the brief but sobering presentation was finally over, Steve was the first to speak up. "I don't know about the rest of you," he declared, "but I'm starving. What say we all go back to our cabins, get dressed for dinner, and meet up in the main dining room in an hour?"

"Anything to get away from all that gloom and doom," whined Angela. "I was beginning to think about jumping board and swimming home."

"You'd never make it," replied Monica. "Sharks would get you before you could swim a hundred yards."

"Nice," laughed Steve. "Let's go back to our room before you scare Angela to death."

"Well, it's the truth, isn't it?"

"Never mind, sweetheart." Steve grabbed Monica's arm and playfully dragged her away.

"Don't pay any attention to Monica," consoled Gilberto. "She means well but sometimes she says things she should not."

"So I've noticed."

"Dinner is at eight. Would you like me to escort you to the dining room?"

"No." Even though he paid for it, there was no way she was letting him inside her cabin. Not tonight or any other night. "I'll just meet you there."

"Whatever suits you," he replied.

"Yeah, whatever," she whispered as he walked away.

Angela had packed her green sundress. It was the only dress she owned but with the recent addition of a sequined Cuban shawl, it took on a whole new look. When she looked in the bathroom's full length mirror, she noticed her pony-tail didn't match her outfit. She pulled the rubber band off, shook her head, and let her silvery locks cascade over her shoulders. The effect was so dramatic it even surprised her. "Not bad for an old bug zapper," she exclaimed. Throwing her head back, she exited her cabin and headed for dinner.

Heads turned as Angela walked through

the dining room. Some people whispered and pointed. It made her feel special to be noticed. She held her head high and smiled as she approached her friends.

"Wow. You look beautiful," gasped Steve.

"Yes, you do," added Gilberto. If one look was as good as a thousand words, he had just recited the Gettysburg Address.

"Well, thank you kind sirs." Angela's confidence level soared. *So this is what it feels like to be beautiful,* she thought.

Apparently jealous at all the attention Angela was receiving, Monica quickly broke the mood. "Not to change the subject or anything, but did you know there was another Peeping Tom incident in the park last night?"

"No. What happened?"

"Liz Chandler was coming home from her aerobics class and when she pulled into her driveway she saw someone run out the back door of her trailer."

"The guy was actually in her trailer?" Angela had forgotten about being beautiful.

"Liz said he didn't take anything but her bed looked like it had been slept in."

"That is terrible," said Gilberto. "Did she call the police?"

"Yes, but they didn't do anything because Liz couldn't give them a description. I guess the guy was dressed head to toe in black and he ran so fast that he disappeared before the cops got there."

"What about Rambo?" asked Angela. "Where was he when all this happened?"

"At home watching TV. Says he didn't see or hear a thing."

"Some security guard," criticized Steve. "Seems like he's never around when he's needed."

"Maybe he should be replaced," suggested Gilberto. "I could talk to the park manager next week."

"I'll go with you," volunteered Steve. "Maybe the two of us together will carry more weight."

"My hero," crooned Monica. "Just wait till I get you out on that dance floor. I'll show you my appreciation."

"You guys are really going dancing tonight?" asked Angela.

"Sure. Aren't you?"

"No. I think I'll just go back to my room after dinner. It's been quite an eventful day and I want to rest up before we go on shore tomorrow."

"Oh, don't be such a party pooper," mocked Monica. "You can rest up when you get home. Tonight is all about music, moonlight, and magic."

"Magic? What magic?"

"You'll never know if you're not there."

Over her better judgment, Angela agreed to join her friends in the disco lounge after dinner. At first, the music was mostly ballads and show tunes but around midnight, it changed to Latin rhythms.

"That's more like it," shouted Monica as she dragged Steve to the dance floor. They danced a mambo, a tango, and two cha-cha-chas one right after the other. When the DJ played a *paso doble,* Steve gave up. "I'm getting too old for this." He breathed heavily as threw himself into a chair.

Gilberto reached over and took Angela's hand. "Come, my beautiful friend. Let us show them how it is done."

"I couldn't," she objected. "I've seen it done on TV but I don't know any of the steps."

"Go on Angela," coaxed Monica. "Just do what comes naturally."

Since it looked like she wasn't going to get out of it, Angela allowed Gilberto to lead her to the dance floor. Hoping no one was watching, she stood to one side as Gil slowly circled her. The look in his eyes and his slow, deliberate movements mesmerized her. When he raised his hands above his head and clapped them together, she snapped her head towards him. When he stomped his foot on the floor, she took hold of her shawl and swirled it in front of her. Her hair fell across her face but it didn't stop her from dancing. Gilberto slid his hand around her waist and they stood face to face for a brief moment. Then Angela pulled away, defiantly stared at Gilberto, and stomped her foot.

"Will you look at that?" laughed Monica. "And she just wanted to go back to her room."

As the music grew louder, Angela and Gilberto's movements became more dramatic. They dipped. They twirled. They spun. They moved in and then away from each other. He was the matador. She was the cape. Together, they owned the floor.

When the music finally ended, Gilberto took Angela in his arms and kissed her. Letting her shawl drag on the floor, she turned and pranced slowly off the dance floor.

16
REVELATIONS

Angela barely put her suitcase down when the phone started ringing. "I want EVERY detail."

"Hello, Katherine. How's my dog?" Gizmo spent two nights with Katherine and Mongo while Angela was away. Hopefully, it hadn't left a lasting effect.

"You're dog is fine. In fact, I think he's in love with my boyfriend. Can you sue an animal for alienation of affections?"

"Not likely." *Even if you could,* thought Angela, *why would you?* Mongo wasn't that good of a catch.

"So what happened? Did you and Gilberto . . . you know?"

"If you mean what I think you mean, no, we did not. And where do you get off asking me a personal question like that?" Angela tried to act indignant but the whole idea of a budding romance brought a smile to her face.

"I'm your best friend. Best friends have privileges."

"So we're best friends, are we?"

"If you don't tell me about your trip, I'll come over there and beat it out of you."

"Everything was wonderful. My stateroom was bigger and fancier than my trailer and the food was out of this world. Gil even complimented the chef and you know how fussy he is."

"Yes . . . yes . . ."

"We all went on shore Saturday morning and I got to see the Blue Lagoon. You know . . . where they filmed the movie?"

"Who cares about lagoons and movies? Did anything happen between you and Gil?" Katherine emphasized every syllable.

"As a matter of fact, yes. He kissed me."

"And . . ."

"And that's all. We went dancing the first night and did the *paso doble*."

"The what?"

"The *paso doble*. It's a spicy Latin dance that is supposed to resemble a bullfight."

"Where'd you learn that?" Katherine sounded like a shocked schoolmarm.

"I don't know. Probably one of those celebrity dancing shows." Angela enjoyed stringing her friend along.

"Forget about the dancing. What about

the kiss?"

"Well, when the music ended Gil sort of tipped me backwards. You know — in a dip? Then he kissed me."

"That's it? He just kissed you?"

"Yes. What did you expect? A proposal of marriage or something?"

"Well, something. Did he invite you back to his room?"

"Of course not. He's a gentleman."

"Oh, don't give me that. Men are men."

"Well, he's a gentleman with me." Angela wondered if Gil had ever made at pass at Katherine. Probably not. Somehow the two of them together didn't paint a pretty picture — more like Rocky Horror than The Sound of Music.

"Next thing you're gonna tell me is he doesn't have a crush on you."

"That's ridiculous, Katherine. We're just good friends."

"Sure. Just like Bill and Monica."

"Listen, Katherine. I'd love to let you delve further into my personal life but I've got a lot of things to do. Can I come over in a little while and pick up Gizmo?"

"Oh, all right," she answered reluctantly. "I'll let you off the hook for now but I want a full report when you get here."

"Does it have to be notarized?"

"Smart aleck. Hey, why don't you come for dinner? Mongo is making fajitas."

"I thought he was Cuban."

"He is. He adds plantains to his fajitas."

"Yuk. I think I'll pass."

"No, really, they're good. Be here around six. You'll see."

"I can hardly wait."

The minute Angela laid down the phone, it rang again.

"Good Grief, Katherine, give me a break."

"It's Fran, Angela. Tony is in the hospital."

Without waiting for details, Angela jumped into her car and raced for the hospital. Sunday afternoon traffic was heavy but she managed to cover the twelve miles in fifteen minutes. Pulling into the lot, she parked in a handicap spot and ran into the hospital.

A white-haired woman was sitting at the reception desk knitting what appeared to be baby booties.

"May I help you?" asked the woman.

"Yes, please. Can you tell me what room Tony Dunn is in?"

"Certainly." The woman quickly typed Tony's name into the computer on her desk. "Four thirty five," she replied cheerfully. "Would you like to buy a pair of baby booties?" She held the booties up for Angela's inspection. "They're for the orphans in the nursery."

Angela wondered why the woman was bothering her with baby booties. Couldn't she see she had more important things on her mind? She hurriedly dug through her purse and pulled out a five-dollar bill. "Is this enough?" she asked.

"Oh, that's so generous," replied the woman. "Most people just give me a dollar."

Angela just shrugged and walked toward the elevators. Riding up to the fourth floor, she felt a little guilty about being so rude to the woman. After all, she was just trying to do something nice for the orphans. If she saw her again, she should probably apologize.

When the elevator doors opened, Angela was surprised to see Fran standing there. "I'm going downstairs for a cigarette. Want to join me?"

"What about Tony?" Angela held the elevator doors open with one hand.

"He's stable. The doctor is with him right now so you won't be able to see him for a while." Fran stepped into the elevator.

"What happened?" asked Angela as she let the doors close.

"Same as last time. He drank too much

and passed out. Only this time the para-medics said he might have had a heart at-tack."

A look of concern crossed Angela's face. "Both our parents had heart conditions."

"I know. That's what's got me worried."

They stepped outside the hospital and walked a short distance away from the doors. "So what actually happened?" asked Angela.

"Well, he started drinking early this morn-ing and was passed out on the couch by ten o'clock. I thought he was sleeping it off so I left him alone. When I couldn't wake him up for lunch, I called the paramedics. They said his blood sugar was dangerously low and that he had gone into a coma. They gave him oxygen and put him on an IV. He opened his eyes and mumbled that he was okay but the paramedics insisted he go to the hospital. One of them said the doctors would run some tests to determine if he had a heart attack."

"Has this happened before?"

"Last Thanksgiving, as you already know, and two times before that."

"Two times? Do the doctors know what's causing it?"

"They say he has diabetes and that he shouldn't drink but he refuses to take medication or give up drinking."

"He could die."

Fran dropped her spent cigarette on the ground, smashed it with her shoe, and immediately lit another. "I know."

"What are you going to do?" Angela's voice cracked.

"What can I do? I'll keep bugging him to quit drinking but aside from that, he's in God's hands."

"Can I help?"

"Your being here is a big help. Tony probably won't be able to go back to work for a couple of weeks. Can you handle the business?"

"Of course I can. If need be, I'll get Steve and Gilberto to help. Maybe even Rambo."

"I wouldn't count on Rambo." Fran finished her second cigarette and lit a third.

"Why not?"

"He was arrested last night."

"What for?" laughed Angela.

"They found him sneaking around Liz Chandler's trailer. Guess he actually broke into it a couple of days ago. Anyway, Liz sprayed him with mace then called the cops. He was sitting on the ground rubbing his eyes and crying like a baby when the squad pulled up."

"Do they think he's the Peeping Tom?"

"Oh, yeah. He even confessed. Said he never meant to hurt anyone, just liked being around pretty things."

"That's creepy. Guess I was lucky just getting a rose. I don't think I'd be able to sleep in my trailer again if I knew he'd been inside."

"Katherine said Mongo was upset because Rambo never went back to their place. He had a trap set up in case he came sneaking around."

"Rambo might be dumb but he certainly isn't stupid. I'm sure he knows better than to mess with a Cuban."

"So true."

"Any idea how long he'll be in jail?"

"He couldn't come up with bail so he'll probably be there a while. If we're lucky, someone will throw away the key."

"Dream on."

"So what do ya say? Ready to go up and see your brother?"

"Sure. Let's do it."

When Angela and Fran walked into Tony's room, he was laying on the bed with his eyes closed.

"Is he still in a coma?" Angela looked around the room. Nowhere near as luxurious as the one he had been in on Thanksgiving, this room's purpose seemed obvious

— saving Tony's life. Several large machines with read-out monitors beeped noisily and two IV bags hung from a chrome shepherd's hook standing nearby.

"No," mumbled Tony. "I'm awake."

"How are you feeling, honey?" Fran gently rubbed Tony's hand.

"Lousy. I've got a horrible headache and I ache from all the needles they've been poking into me." It sounded as if he was losing his voice.

"What did the doctor say?"

"Not much."

"Does he know if you had a heart attack?"

"He said he wouldn't know anything until he gets the tests back."

"When will that be?" asked Angela.

"Sometime tomorrow. In the meantime, I've got to stay here."

"Do you need anything?" asked Fran. "Pajamas? Shaving kit? Magazines?"

"No, I'm fine. But I would like to talk to Angela for a minute. Do you mind?"

"Whatever you want, Tony," replied Fran. "I'll go down the hall and look for a coffee machine. Want one Angela?"

"Sure. Thanks Fran."

Tony and Angela watched as Fran left the room then Tony motioned for Angela to sit on the bed.

"What's up?" asked Angela.

"I had a close call this time and it's made me think about a lot of things."

"Like what, Tony?" Angela tried to keep her mood cheerful even though she knew this was going to be one of those serious talks most people try to avoid.

"Like I haven't been exactly straight with you lately." He shifted his body, obviously looking for a comfortable position.

"You know, maybe it would be better if we talked when you got home." Even though Angela's curiosity was driving her crazy, she was concerned about where the conversation was headed.

"No. I need to get this off my chest right now." Tony took a deep breath and confessed. "I called Carl."

"Why? Were you afraid you were dying?" Trying to get some meaning from his words, Angela studied her brother's face.

"No. Nothing like that. I asked him to come down here and take you home."

Angela leaped from the bed like a Jack springing from its box. "What do you mean home?"

"Indiana."

"Why would I want to go back there?"

"Because you don't have anything here."

"That's not true. I've got you and Fran."

"Listen, Sis. If something happens to me Fran would probably move back to Tennessee to be with her family. What would you do?"

"I don't know. Stay here. Keep the business going. Maybe buy a house? Anything but go back to Indiana. And certainly not to the jerk I used to call my husband."

"Carl isn't so bad."

"You didn't have to live with him." Angela turned her back to Tony and looked out the window. *What would I do,* she wondered? *I gave up everything to come down here and once the doctor returns and takes back his trailer, I'll have nothing. And if something happens to Tony, I'll have no one to turn to.*

"He said he was sorry about how he treated you and that he really wants you back."

"Yeah? What happened to his wonderful yoga instructor? Did she find someone younger?" Tears were rolling down Angela's cheeks but she looked up at the ceiling and kept her voice strong.

"Don't be so tough on the guy, Angela. Give him a break."

Angela turned to face her brother. "When did you and Carl become such good buddies? Was it before or after I moved down here?"

"We're not buddies, Angela. I just think it would be better if you had someone to look after you."

"And you think that should be Carl?"

"Who else is there?"

"I've got friends."

"Oh, yeah. A lecherous old cook, a crazy redhead, and a couple of Peace Corps rejects. You call those friends?"

"You know what, Tony? I don't want to say anything that will upset you so I think I'll just say goodbye and go home."

"What's the matter? Can't take the truth?"

"Goodbye, Tony." Angela stormed out the door just as Fran came in.

"Whoa. What's wrong?" asked Fran as she stepped out of Angela's way.

"Ask your husband."

Angela reached the parking lot just in time to see her car being towed away from the handicap zone. She closed her eyes, threw her head back and screamed as loud as she could.

17
CARL

Angela was giving Gilberto's front door a second coat of paint when Carl drove up and honked the horn.

"Hey, good looking," he yelled. "I didn't know you could paint."

Without putting the paintbrush down, Angela turned her head. The voice was familiar but the car was not. She shaded her eyes to get a better look.

"Don't you recognize your own husband?" he asked.

"I'm not married and haven't been for more than fifteen years." She felt less than happy to see Carl and didn't make any attempt to hide it.

"Seventeen to be exact," replied Carl as he stepped out of the car. "But who's counting?"

"Me," she snapped. "They were the best years of my life."

"Oh, don't be that way, Angela. I drove a

long way to come and see you."

"Go find Tony. He's the one who invited you down here."

"Look, I know you're not happy to see me and I can guess why. But a lot of things have happened in my life and I'd like to tell you about them."

"I'm not interested." Nothing Carl Singer could say was going to make any difference.

"Come on, Angela, all I need is an hour."

"Can't you see I'm busy?" Angela frowned and waved the paintbrush.

"Oh. Sure. I'm sorry. How about later? We could go to dinner or something."

Even though she didn't like the idea of having dinner with him, Angela knew if she didn't give in Carl wouldn't go away. Heaving a deep sigh, she threw the paintbrush into the bucket and reluctantly agreed. "Where are you staying?"

"Down the road at the Palms. They've got a halfway decent restaurant. We could eat there." His smile looked painted on.

"I'll call you after I finish here. Now if you don't mind, I've got work to do." Angela watched Carl drive away. When he was well out of sight she turned around, leaned her head against the door, and pounded her fists on it.

Gilberto had been standing inside listening to the whole exchange. When he heard the commotion, he stepped outside. "What are you doing, Angela? You just painted that door." He tried to wipe the paint from her forehead but she pulled away.

"I don't care," she screeched.

Gilberto wrapped his arms around her. "Come inside and calm down. I will make you some tea."

"I don't want tea, Gil. I just want to be left alone." As she started to walk away, she kicked the paint bucket sending terra cotta paint splashing down the steps and on Gilberto's shoes.

"Would you like me to walk you home?" He ignored the paint but left footprints with every step he took.

"No. I'll be all right. I just need time to think."

"Call me if you need anything," he said worriedly.

When Angela reached her trailer she practically ripped the screen door off its hinges. Gizmo came running when he heard her at the door but she was in no mood for his antics. "Get down," she shouted when he jumped to greet her. The dog flattened his ears and crept away.

"What makes that jerk think he can just waltz back into my life after seventeen years?" She had a lot of frustration to get rid of and it seemed the best way to do that was by yelling. "Everything was going so well for me. I've got a new job, new friends, and a whole new life. I'm finally getting my act together. I don't need an ex-husband messing it up." She grabbed the refrigerator door to get something cold to drink and noticed her hand left paint smudges. "Great. What else is gonna go wrong?"

Gizmo crawled out of hiding and rubbed against Angela's leg. Looking down, she noticed his flattened ears. She sat on the floor and nuzzled his head. "Oh, Gizmo, what am I going to do? Should I tell him I'm sick and can't have dinner with him?"

The dog hung his head.

"You're right. That won't work. He'd probably bring dinner here and I really don't want him to see where we live."

The dog tilted his head as if asking what was wrong with their home.

"I could say I already had other plans but all he'd have to do is drive by to see that wasn't true. What if I told him I had a jealous boyfriend?"

Gizmo smiled.

"Knowing him, he'd just laugh and make a fool out of me. Darn you, Tony. Why did you do this to me?"

As if on cue, the phone rang. Angela jumped to her feet and grabbed it. "What?" she demanded.

"Wow. Sounds like someone's having a bad day," observed Katherine.

"The worst. Carl is in town."

"Your ex?"

"The one and only," sighed Angela.

"What's he doing here?"

"Tony called him."

"You're kidding."

"Why would I kid about a thing like that?" Angela sometimes wondered if all that red dye had affected her friend's brain.

"So what does he want?"

"He says he has something to tell me."

"Like what?"

"I haven't got a clue. He wants to go to dinner so we can talk." Angela picked at some crumbs on the kitchen counter. Realizing she hadn't eaten since breakfast she started rummaging through the overhead cabinet.

"Are you going?"

"Not if I can help it." There were canned beans, dry pasta, and a bottle of spicy mustard in the cabinet. What she really wanted was chocolate.

"I think you should go."

Angela stared at the phone. "Are you serious?" She practically spit the words out.

"Yes. You've been carrying around a lot of repressed anger and this might be the perfect opportunity to get rid of it."

"Well, thank you Dr. Phil." Finding a chocolate cake mix, Angela tore the box open, tipped her head back, and tapped the bottom of the box to force some of its contents into her mouth. Unfortunately, she tapped too hard and scattered chocolate cake mix all over her chin, the phone, and the front of her paint smudged t-shirt.

"Think about it, Angela. That good-for-nothing hurt you and you've been leery of men ever since. You won't even let Gil get close to you."

"That's ridiculous." Angela pushed the cake mix away and tried to wipe her shirt clean.

"Is it? Then why do you keep him at arm's length?"

She wondered if she was really doing that. "I don't know how long I'll be in Florida and I don't want to start something I'm not going to finish."

"Now that's a pretty lame excuse. You made friends with me and Mongo didn't you?"

"That's different."

"No it isn't. Kick that scum ball out of

your life so you can start enjoying yourself for a change."

"I don't know . . ."

"Just do it, Angela."

"Maybe you're right."

"Of course I am. Have you ever known me to be wrong?"

"Well, there was that one time . . ."

"Oh, hush up and listen. The reason I called was to invite you for coffee and dessert later this evening."

"Why? Is it your birthday or something?" Birthdays meant cake and cake meant chocolate.

"No, it is not. I just thought it would be a nice thing to do."

"Come on, Katherine, I know you better than that. You don't do things just because they're nice. What's up?"

"You'll find out when you get here. How's eight?"

"Do I have a choice?"

"Of course not."

"Oh, all right. I'll probably need something gooey after meeting with Carl anyway."

"So you're going tonight?"

"I guess."

"Good girl. Give that sleazoid a piece of your mind. And some of mine, too, while you're at it."

"Yeah. Sure."

"Oh, and Angela? Good luck."

"Thanks. I think I'm gonna need it."

Angela threw the half empty cake mix into the garbage, took a quick shower, pulled her hair into a ponytail, and put on a cotton blouse and clean cutoffs. There was no way she was going to get gussied up for Carl — not after what he had done to her. She fed and walked Gizmo, called Carl to say she was on her way, and asked God to give her strength for what lay ahead.

When she arrived at the hotel, she was surprised to find Carl standing out front, wearing a suit and tie and holding a grocery store bouquet of flowers. "Oh, swell," she muttered. "This is gonna be worse than I expected." Before she had a chance to remove the keys from the ignition, Carl opened her car door.

"I've been watching for you." He handed her the flowers and gasped when he saw her cutoffs. "I thought we were going to dinner."

"We are," she replied sarcastically. "Everyone dresses casually down here. Guess we're not as high-class as all you folks up there in Kokomo." She stepped out of the car, slammed the door, and led the way.

Once inside the restaurant, the maitre d' seated them at a back table. Wondering if it had anything to do with the way she was dressed, Angela snickered. *Serves Carl right,* she thought. *It's about time someone put him in his place.*

After looking at the menus and placing their orders, Carl wasted no time. Taking hold of Angela's hand and gazing into her eyes he asked, "Have you ever done anything you wished you could take back?"

Angela laughed and jerked her hand away. "Yes — this dinner."

Carl laced his fingers together as if in prayer. "I've done a lot of bad things in my life, Angela, and hurting you was the worst." He almost whimpered.

Even though Carl was finally saying the words she'd waited to hear for seventeen years, Angela wondered why he was saying them now. What was his angle?

"We had the perfect life," he continued. "The farm . . . the clean air . . . the animals. We could have been healthy and happy. But no, I had to go and ruin everything."

Not knowing whether to laugh or cry, Angela said the first thing that came to her mind. "Yes, you did. But why bring it up now?"

"I started going to church about five years

ago and it made me take a good long look at myself. I didn't like what I saw, Angela. I was a very selfish and materialistic man. I used other people to get what I wanted then once I got it, I tossed them away. I was a liar, a cheat, and a philanderer. Everything and everyone was fair game. Then I found God."

Once again, Carl reached for Angela's hand. She didn't pull away. They fell in love all those years ago. Maybe a trace of that love still burned somewhere in his heart.

"God showed me the way, Angela. I quit taking advantage of people, I gave up drinking, smoking, and chasing women, and I even started doing volunteer work at a local mission. I changed my life and God forgave me my sins. Do you think you could ever find it in your heart to forgive me?"

The waiter placed their dinners on the table. Angela had ordered a salad and Carl pasta. Neither one of them seemed very interested in eating.

Angela shook her head. "This is all so sudden, Carl. I don't know what to say."

"Then don't say anything. Let's just enjoy our dinners and each other's company."

Angela stared down at her salad, pushed an anemic cherry tomato to the side, and asked the question that was bothering her.

"Are you saying we should get back together?"

"Yes, Angela, I am. You were the best thing that ever happened to me and I was a fool to let you go."

Fifteen years ago Angela would have jumped at a chance like this, now she wasn't so sure. Past experience warned her not to believe Carl. But what if he was telling the truth? What if he had really changed and wanted to start a new life with her? Could all those years of heartache just be forgotten like they'd never happened? She felt her resolve melting.

"You worked a number on me, Carl. Why should I trust you now?"

"I know I hurt you, Angela, but I never stopped loving you."

Angela covered her eyes and rested her forehead in her hands.

"Are you all right?" asked Carl.

"Actually, I'm not very hungry. If you don't mind, I think I'd like to go home."

"I'll drive you."

"No, that won't be necessary."

"I insist," he argued. "I'll take you home then call a cab to bring me back here."

As they drove into the trailer park, Angela suddenly remembered she had promised to stop at Katherine's house. "She'll never forgive me if I don't show up. I think it's her birthday or something. Would you mind dropping me off there?"

"I'll go with you," suggested Carl. "That way I can meet some of your friends."

Even though she knew it wasn't a good idea, Angela didn't have the strength to argue. "Okay, but we'll only stay a few minutes."

"Whatever you want, Angela." Carl grinned as he parked the car and ran around to open Angela's door. Taking her by the arm, he gently led her up to Katherine's front door.

Opening the door, Katherine immediately assessed the situation. "Wow. You look like death warmed over. Did something not agree with you?" Her suspicious eyes bore holes into Carl's skull.

"I'm fine," muttered Angela. "Just a little tired." She looked around the room and noticed Steve and Monica snuggling on the sofa. She started to walk toward them but was stopped in her tracks.

"Aren't you going to introduce your friend?" insisted Katherine.

"I'm sorry. This is my . . . this is Carl Singer. From Kokomo."

"We've heard a lot about you, Carl Singer," sneered Katherine.

"Well, we're not all perfect," cracked Carl.

A knock at the door ended the frosty banter.

"Gee, I wonder who that could be." Katherine smirked as she opened the door. Gilberto stood in the doorway holding two dozen white roses and a magnum of champagne.

"Congratulations." He walked into the room and gave Katherine a peck on the cheek. When he looked about to do the same to Angela, she shook her head and turned away.

"Thank you, Gil," replied Katherine. "Have a seat. We were just about to begin."

"Begin what?" asked Monica.

"Mongo and I invited all of you here tonight for a very special announcement."

"You're not pregnant, are you?" joked Steve.

"No, wise guy, I'm not. Mongo and I have finally decided to get married."

"It took you long enough," shouted Steve.

"Well, if it hadn't have been for you and Monica we probably would never have done it." Katherine laughed as she handed everyone a champagne glass.

"You mean we shamed you into it?" asked Monica.

"Yeah. Something like that. You always

said marriage was a sacred occupation so we decided to give it a try."

Gilberto opened the champagne and filled everyone's glass. *"Alla coppia felice,"* he announced as he raised his glass.

"What's that supposed to mean?" jeered Carl.

"It means good luck to the happy couple." Gilberto was obviously trying to remain cordial.

"So why didn't you just say that?"

Gilberto offered his hand to Carl. *"Bon giorno, senore.* My name is Gilberto Fontero."

"What are you? Italian or something?" Carl didn't offer his hand back.

"Si. From Naples. And you are . . . ?"

"I'm Angela's husband."

"I believe the correct term is ex-husband," replied Gilberto coldly.

"Not for long." Carl put his arm around Angela's shoulders as if showing possession.

"Angela, what is this man talking about?" Gilberto looked like he was beginning to lose control.

"None of your business," replied Carl.

"Angela is my business," protested Gilberto.

"Not anymore." Carl turned Angela away from Gilberto.

The room became silent. Everyone seemed to know what was going to happen next.

Gilberto grabbed Carl by the shoulder; Carl whipped around and swung at Gilberto; Gilberto laid a right hook across Carl's nose.

"Stop it, both of you," screamed Angela. Tears stained her cheeks as she struggled with deciding which man to side with.

Moaning in pain, Carl wiggled his nose to see if it was broken. There was a crackling sound and he pulled away bloody fingers. Angela grabbed a napkin from the table and tried to stop the bleeding.

Gilberto approached Angela with outstretched hands. "I am so sorry, Angela."

Helping Carl toward the front door, she turned and shrieked at Gilberto. "Stay out of my life, Gilberto Fontero. I never want to see you again. Do you understand?"

Angela had made her decision.

18
STORM WARNINGS

Even though the emergency room doctor told Carl he would live, Angela took it upon herself to nurse him back to health. After all, if he hadn't come to Florida to see her, his nose would never have been broken. It was all her fault and she had to do something to make it up to him. So rather than sending him back to his lonely hotel room, she let him take over her bedroom while she and Gizmo slept on the sun porch. She didn't go to work, talk to her any of her friends, or turn on the radio or television. She put her life on hold. Carl was the only thing that mattered.

Carl, of course, took full advantage of Angela's self-inflicted guilt. He complained that the doctor hadn't packed his nose correctly; he talked about the possibility of permanent disfigurement or never being able to breathe right; he took Ibuprofen by the fistful. Every time Angela looked at his bandaged nose and blackened eyes, she nearly broke into tears. But after three days of fetching icepacks, cooking homemade chicken soup, and catering to her ex-husband's every whim, her nerves were on edge.

One morning while Angela was preparing Carl's breakfast, the phone rang. She turned the heat off under the French toast and grabbed the receiver.

"Good morning, Mrs. Singer. This is Ed Morris, Carl's real estate agent. Is he available?"

Rather than debate the "Mrs." issue, Angela simply replied that Carl was in the shower.

"Ask him to give me a call when he gets out. I worked out a pretty sweet deal on the property he wants to buy and we need to go over a few details."

"Property?"

"Yes, the old Tucker estate out on Redbud Road. Two hundred and fifty acres of the prettiest farmland in the area. I'll bet you're really excited."

"Ah . . . yeah, I am. I'll have him call you. Does he have your number?"

"Well, I should hope so. We've been working on this deal for six months. Tell him we need to act quickly. The Tucker family is considering another offer."

Angela hung up the phone and fell into a kitchen chair. What was going on? Had Carl started thinking about a farm before or after Tony called him? And how did she figure into all this? Before she had time to sort things out, Carl entered the room.

Rubbing a towel to his wet hair, Carl walked up to the stove and sniffed. "Mmmm, smells good. But why'd you turn the heat off?"

"The phone rang and I got distracted."

"Oh yeah? Anyone I know?"

"As a matter of fact, yes. Someone named Ed Morris. Said he's your real estate agent."

"No kidding. What else did he say?"

"Just that he worked out a deal on the Tucker place and wants you to call him." She tried to keep her voice calm but her frustration seeped through. "What's going on, Carl?"

"No need to get your feathers ruffled, Angela. I was gonna tell you all about it but your slug-happy boyfriend broke my nose before I had a chance to say anything."

"Gilberto isn't my boyfriend."

"Really? He seems to think so."

"Well, he's not, so quit trying to change the subject. What made you decide to buy another farm?"

"I wanted us to get back to the way we were in the beginning. You know — the farm, the animals, the whole works. Things will be the way they were supposed to be."

"But the Tucker place? If I remember right, it's huge. Can you afford it?"

"Not me, Angela. Us. The farm will be ours and with our combined salaries, we'll be able to swing it."

Angela's stomach dropped to the floor. There it was — the angle. Carl didn't care about her; he had just been using her to get what he wanted. His trip to Florida was nothing but a ruse. How could she have been so naive? But what if he had really changed and was telling the truth about wanting them to get back together? A farm would be nice. She could raise goats and chickens and rescue as many dogs as she wanted. Maybe she could even turn the farm into one big animal shelter. She didn't know what to think.

"I need to clear my head, Carl. I'm going for a walk."

"What about my breakfast?"

Angela stared at Carl's swollen face. Did she even know him? "I'm sorry, Carl. I have to get out of here."

She grabbed Gizmo by the collar and led him to the car. She'd go to the beach — the smell of the sea air always calmed her. Halfway there, she realized she hadn't brought a leash. "Oh, who cares?" she told the dog. "We'll just sit in the car and watch the waves come in."

The dog jumped into the back seat and wagged his tail. Any time spent with his human was one big glorious adventure even if it only meant going for a ride.

Angela had no trouble finding a parking spot. Aside from a few wave runners in the water, the beach was practically empty. The bikini-clad beauty queens, the oiled body builders, even the ever-present, knee-padded roller bladers were all mysteriously absent.

"Wonder what's going on?" she asked Gizmo.

The dog licked the window.

"Oh, sorry. Guess you want that opened."

He wagged his tail.

When she opened the window, an unexpected gust of wind blasted a shower of sand into the car. "Good grief. That's why no one's around."

Gizmo nervously pulled away from the window and whimpered while Angela rolled it up and reached for the radio. "Well, if we can't smell the ocean, at least we can listen to some music and watch it."

She pushed her favorite station button but instead of soft jazz, she got hard news: "At nine a.m. eastern daylight time, the center of hurricane Damian was located near latitude 21.4 north, longitude 79.9 west or about two hundred and fifty miles south-southeast of Key West, Florida. While some wobbling has occurred, Damian is expected to continue moving toward the northwest at thirty-five miles per hour. On this track, the center should make landfall along the eastern coast of Florida by late this afternoon. Reconnaissance aircraft data indicate maximum sustained winds have increased to near one hundred and fifty miles per hour. Damian is a strong category four hurricane on the Saffir-Simpson scale. Some weakening is forecast as the storm moves over Cuba but it is expected to remain a major hurricane as it emerges over the southeastern Gulf of Mexico today. Damian is expected to produce total rainfall accumulations of four to eight inches over the entire east coast of Florida. These rains could produce life-threatening flash floods and mud slides."

A hurricane was coming and it was headed her way. What should she do? Should she go home and warn Carl? Should she go to Tony's? Should she go to Katherine's or

Gilberto's? Barely able to catch her breath, she threw the car into reverse and sped out of the parking lot.

Her first thought was of Carl so she raced home only to find him sitting in front of the television with a can of soda in his hand and a box of chocolate donuts sitting on the table in front of him.

"Hey, look at this." Carl pointed his soda at the screen. "They just issued a hurricane warning. How cool is that?"

"Is that your idea of breakfast?" She wanted to throw the donuts across the room.

"You ran out on me so I raided the refrigerator. By the way, your donuts are stale."

Carl didn't mention whether he had called his real estate agent and Angela didn't ask. All she could think about was the hurricane. "Forget the donuts, hurricanes are destructive, and they scare me."

"Don't worry about a thing, Babe. I'm here to protect you."

Angela wasn't so sure. "Well, just in case, I'm gonna call someone who knows a little more about them than you."

"Whatever," mocked Carl. "Just let me know when it's time to run for cover." He laughed and started flipping the channels.

Angela was furious. She'd raced all the

way back from the beach because she was worried about Carl and there he was, sitting in her living room, eating her donuts, and laughing about the hurricane. She grabbed the phone and dialed Katherine's number. The woman might have been a scatter-brained redhead but she'd probably been through enough hurricanes to know what to do.

"Have you heard the news?" she asked when Katherine answered.

"What? The hurricane? Don't worry about that silly thing, it's a hundred miles away and it'll probably shift course way before it gets here."

"What if it doesn't?"

"Then we'll have a hurricane party."

"A what?"

"A hurricane party. We have them every year."

"You're kidding — right?" What was wrong with people? First Carl and now Katherine. Didn't they know how danger-ous hurricanes could be?

"Seriously, they're great fun. Last year I had one when Lamont was headed this way. Everyone cleaned out their refrigerator and we had a great big pot luck dinner."

"Why did they clean out their refrigera-tors?" Angela thought her friend had finally lost her mind.

"We usually lose power during a hurricane so we decided to get rid of all the perishables before they could go bad."

"Weren't you worried about getting hurt?" If it had been her, she would have been hiding in a closet or under a bed.

"There's not much you can do about a hurricane so you might as well enjoy yourself while you can."

"Well, that's pretty depressing," groaned Angela.

"It's the truth," replied Katherine. "Hurricanes are unpredictable — just like life. You've got to learn to chill out. Know what I mean?"

"All I know is that I want nothing to do with them. Is there some sort of shelter or someplace we can go to get away from it?" If she'd never moved to Florida, none of this would have been happening.

"You could call Steve. He usually knows about things like that."

"Thanks, I'll call him right now."

"Say 'Hi' from me," chirped Katherine.

Angela hung up and immediately dialed Steve who seemed a little more understanding. "The first thing you should do is get your trailer boarded up."

"How do I do that?"

"Go to the Home Depot and buy enough plywood to cover all the doors and windows then nail it up. The plywood helps keep flying debris from breaking your windows and getting inside your trailer."

"That happens?" She wondered how bad things were going to get.

"Oh, sure. And once the windows are broken, the rain can come in. Sometimes the rain causes more damage than the wind."

"Is my roof safe?" Angela envisioned the trailer's tin roof flying down the highway.

"If things get that bad you need to get out of there." Steve wasn't sugarcoating anything.

"Where should I go?"

"Your best bet is the National Guard Armory."

"Where's that?" Angela felt panic setting in.

"Don't worry, Angela," replied Steve. "I'll call you way before anything like that happens. Monica and I will even drive you there."

"Really?" With a priest and nun on her side, what could go wrong?

"Of course. What are friends for?"

Angela swallowed hard but didn't say anything. She remembered some of those programs she'd watched about hurricanes but it wasn't until that moment that the reality hit home. Trees could be uprooted. Power lines could be knocked down. The doctor's trailer could be destroyed. Even worse — people could die. If she made it through this thing alive, she swore she would pack up and move back to Kokomo with Carl. Gladly.

Obviously sensing her fear, Steve tried to change the subject. "Has Carl left yet?"

"No. He's still here." Somehow, that didn't reassure her.

"Good. He can help with the plywood. And remember . . . if you need anything at all, Monica and I are here for you."

"Thanks, Steve. I really appreciate your help."

Angela turned to Carl and told him what Steve said.

"What does he know?" asked Carl. "I think we should just pack up and hop on the first plane outta here."

"I can't do that, Carl. I promised to take care of this trailer and that's what I'm going to do. Besides, they won't let Gizmo on an airplane."

"Sounds like you're worried more about that dog than me."

You might be right, thought Angela. "I'm

going to Home Depot. Are you coming?"

"Nope. I think I'll just stay here and watch the boob tube."

"Well, do me a favor and take care of Gizmo. He seemed a little nervous when we were at the beach." Carl took a bite from his donut and waved as Angela walked out the door.

It was like a feeding frenzy at Home Depot. Customers were loading up carts and baskets with plywood, paneling, hammers, nails, generators, sand, bungee cords, and batteries — anything they could get their hands on. Most of the shelves were already empty and people were pushing each other around to get what little was left. Angela grabbed what she needed and headed for the checkout lanes.

An old woman carrying a potted plant pushed her way into line in front of Angela. "I've just got this one thing. You don't mind, do you, Dearie?" Even though the woman wasn't wearing her tinfoil cap, Angela recognized Mrs. Snodgrass. Where was her son and why was she buying a plant?

Gilberto walked up and took the woman by the elbow. "Come on, Marion, we have to go to the end of the line."

Angela's heart skipped a beat. While everyone else was running around worried about how they were going to survive, there was Gil, helping out some poor old woman who didn't seem to understand what was going on. If he had been like Carl, he probably would have pushed the woman out of the way.

Gilberto smiled but made no attempt to start a conversation. *Just as well,* thought Angela. *I wouldn't know what to say anyway.*

When Angela got back home, Tony was nailing plywood on her windows.

"I thought you could use a hand," he muttered.

"What's the matter? Couldn't you get your buddy Carl to help?"

"Carl's not here, Angela."

"What do you mean not here? I just left him an hour ago."

"He called me right after you left and said you were being unreasonable about not leaving with him. I told him I thought you were right and he said we were both crazy. Then he called a cab and went to the airport."

Angela stared at her brother in disbelief.

"I'm so sorry, Angela. I should never have interfered in your life. You always told me Carl was no good but I never thought he'd run off and abandon you."

"He's done it before. Why should things

be different now?" Angela realized that the only people left to help her were her brother and a few friends. Would that be enough? She leaned against her car and sighed.

"Is there anything I can do?" asked Tony.

"Yeah. Help me unload this junk. By the way, where'd you get the plywood?" She pointed at the covered windows.

"Jeff keeps a supply in his shed. Most of us do. Come on, I'll show you how to put it up."

Tony and Angela worked side by side for more than an hour. When all the plywood was up, Angela stood back and checked everything over. "Looks like we're ready for whatever comes this way."

"Are you frightened?" asked Tony.

"Sure. Aren't you?"

"Not that I'll ever admit," laughed Tony. "Say . . . think you could rustle up a cold beer for your big brother?"

"Sorry, don't have any."

"What? You giving it up?"

Angela shrugged her shoulders. "Pretty much."

"Why?"

"I don't know. Maybe because I saw how it can affect people."

Tony glared at his sister. "You mean like me?"

"Not just you. Me, too. If I hadn't have been drinking I probably wouldn't have gotten this crazy tattoo." Angela pointed at her ankle.

"Well, don't go off the deep end. I wouldn't want anyone thinking my sister was as teetotaler. Might be bad for my reputation. Know what I mean?"

Angela kiddingly punched Tony in the shoulder. "Like that ever bothered you. How about coffee? Will that do?"

"If that's all you've got."

"It is." Angela surveyed the ply-wooded trailer. "Hey — where's the door?"

Tony showed Angela how to get back into the trailer. Once inside, she filled the coffeemaker then called Gizmo. "Come on out, boy. I've got a cookie for you."

When the dog didn't come running, Angela knew something was wrong. "The wind scared him so much he's probably hiding somewhere."

She looked from room to room. He was nowhere in sight. Running to the living room, she found Tony standing in front of the television. "The governor has ordered a mandatory evacuation," he said. "Come on, let's get Fran, and get out of here."

"I can't leave without Gizmo," protested Angela.

"He'll be all right, Angela. Animals have a sixth sense about things like this."

"But he's practically blind. What if he gets hit by a car or something?"

"Angela, please. We have to go . . . NOW."

19
THE HURRICANE

The merciless rain battered Tony's truck as it idled in bumper-to-bumper traffic on the Interstate. From the looks of it, everyone in south Florida was heading north. Most of the cars were jam packed with kids, dogs, birdcages, and a hodgepodge of boxes, suitcases, and black plastic bags. Anything that didn't fit inside was strapped to the roof. The only cars in the southbound lanes were emergency vehicles and people who looked lost.

Having crawled less than three miles in the last hour, everyone's stress level was increasing as rapidly as the rain and wind. Every once in a while, Fran tried to make small talk but Tony ignored her and Angela just stared out the window wondering if Gizmo had found a safe place to hide.

Tony jerked the wheel and started edging the truck toward the left lane. Several angry drivers honked their horns and tried to block him. When Fran asked what he thought he was doing, he grumbled that he was going to turn around and go home. "We'll be safer there than stuck out here in the open."

"Can we make it?" asked Fran.

"Watch this," he snickered.

Ignoring other drivers' protests, Tony began to force his way toward the median. Small cars were no match against his F150 but an orange Hummer H3X presented more of a problem. The driver, many years younger than Tony, seemed determined to hold his ground. When Tony signaled he wanted to get through, the Hummer driver shook his head, grinned, and took a tighter hold on the steering wheel. As Tony edged closer, the Hummer crept ahead. When the driver in front of the Hummer pulled forward, Tony saw his chance and swerved into the Hummer's lane. Hummer driver rammed Tony's left front wheel well, Fran and Angela screamed, but Tony kept going. The sound of metal on metal filled the cab as he gunned the engine, tore across the flooded median, and bounced into the southbound lanes. The Hummer driver was yelling something but Tony didn't stick around to find out what it was.

Within seconds a squad car roared up

behind Tony's truck and a state trooper on a loudspeaker ordered him to pull over. Tony slammed the gearshift into park and waited as the officer battled the rain.

"Just what did you think you were doing back there?" bellowed the trooper. His plastic-covered hat did little to keep the rain off his face.

Tony rolled down the window and hollered, "Trying to get home." His attitude matched the weather.

"Are you aware there's a mandatory evacuation in effect?"

"Does that look like an evacuation?" Tony jabbed his thumb toward the northbound lanes.

"You're not gonna make it down this road. It's closed down about two miles south of here."

"Well, is there some place I can take my family?"

"Yeah, follow me." The fifty-mile-an-hour wind shoved the trooper back to his vehicle. After struggling to get the squad door open, he jumped in, pulled around Tony's truck, and signaled toward the exit ramp. With lights flashing and siren blaring, he escorted the truck to a large brick building. Even though the arched windows were covered in plywood, the Star of David and Moorish towers above them revealed the building was a synagogue.

"You'll be safe here," shouted the officer. "They've got a basement."

The street was deserted so Tony had no trouble finding a parking spot close to the synagogue entrance. Wrapping one arm around his wife and the other around his sister, he raced into the building, located the stairwell, and hurried to the basement. A bearded man dressed in black greeted them with open arms.

"Come, come," beckoned the man. "We don't have much but we are happy to share."

The man waved his arms around the room. Several military cots with thread-worn blankets and sliver-thin pillows took up one wall while a table filled with cold sandwiches, some sort of noodle casserole, four gallons of purified water, and a large box of candles took up another.

In addition to the bearded man, there were two men, four women, and a handful of children in the room. The men wore black beanies and the women wore shapeless black dresses.

The first man, probably a rabbi, took Angela's hands in his. "You look troubled," he whispered. "Has this storm frightened you?" The man's knuckles were hairy and his palms rough but the gentleness of his voice soothed her.

"Yes," she admitted. "I've never been in a hurricane and I don't know where my dog is." The man's grasp tightened but Angela took strength from it.

"I'm not Jewish or anything but could you say a prayer for him? His name is Gizmo." She swallowed hard.

"Of course."

The bearded man pulled a fringed shawl from beneath his vest, kissed it, and bobbed his head while muttering something in a language Angela once heard when she and Carl attended a Jewish funeral. Not sure of how to act, she bowed her head and closed her eyes as the other two men joined their leader. Then the rabbi translated his prayer.

"Almighty and powerful God, you have given us dominion over all living things. Bless the animals who give us companionship and delight; make us their true friends and worthy companions; and protect all those who may be lost or fearful during this storm."

The three men chanted "Aa-main" in unison.

"Thank you so much," stammered Angela. "That was beautiful."

A sudden crash startled everyone but the

man in black remained calm. "Ruben, stay with the women and children. I will go upstairs and see what has happened."

"I'll go with you," offered Tony.

"No. I think it will be safer if I go alone. If anything happens, do not leave this room until the storm is over."

Before anyone could argue, the rabbi was out the door and headed up the stairs. Two minutes later he returned. "A telephone pole crashed through the sanctuary window and smashed the pulpit. The Eternal Lamp was spared but if the wind keeps up, I am afraid we will soon lose power."

"What will we do then?" asked Angela.

"We will light candles and pray," replied one of the men.

"Like the Festival of Light?" asked Angela.

"Yes," replied the rabbi. "But how do you know about that? I thought you said you weren't Jewish."

"I'm not. My husband, actually my ex-husband, was. He didn't practice his religion but he told me a few things about it."

"What did he tell you about the Festival of Light?"

"Just that it had something to do with Hanukkah and that it was a tradition to light candles before giving out gifts." Her stomach was tied in knots but she tried not to let it show.

"That's part of it," laughed the rabbi, "but there is much more."

"Tell her about the oil," squealed one of the children.

"Hush," silenced the child's mother.

Another crash signaled the storm was gaining strength. This time, the rabbi didn't move.

"Maybe a good story will take everyone's mind off the hurricane," suggested Tony.

"I think you may be right," replied the Rabbi. "And the story of the lamp is particularly appropriate to tell right now. You see, according to the Talmud, our book of laws and history, it all started about two thousand years ago when the Greek-Syrian ruler Antiochus the Fourth tried to force his culture upon the Jews in his territory. He prohibited the practice of the Jewish religion, massacred thousands of Jews, placed a Hellenistic priest in the temple, and desecrated the Temple by sacrificing swine on the altar."

"Pigs?" questioned one of the children.

"Yes, Ephraim," replied the rabbi, "pigs. The vilest and dirtiest of all God's creatures."

"So what did the Jews do?" asked the child.

"Well, although vastly outnumbered, the Jews took up arms to protect their community and their religion. Led by Mattathias the Hasmonean, and later his son Judah the Maccabee, these brave people became known as the Maccabees. After three years of fighting, they victoriously reclaimed and cleansed their beloved temple and prepared it for rededication. Unfortunately, when they went to light the temple lamp for the rededication, they found only enough purified oil to kindle the lamp for a single day. Nevertheless, they used what they had and, miraculously, the light burned for eight days. That was long enough to gather a fresh supply of olive oil and rededicate the temple."

"Hurrah!" shouted the children.

"Yes, hurrah," agreed the Rabbi. "And every year this great event is reenacted during Hanukkah with the lighting of menorahs which have eight lights plus one helper light. Normally, one candle is lit the first night, two the second, and so on. If our lights go out, we will light all the candles and pretend it is the final night of Hanukkah. Look . . . we even have kugal." He pointed to the casserole and everyone laughed.

What courageous people, thought Angela.

All those years ago they lost everything but their faith. Now, here in this basement, they could lose everything again but that didn't stop them from laughing. What kept them going? What gave them strength?

A wrenching sound ripped through the building and the lights went out. It was only two in the afternoon but the room suddenly turned as dark as midnight. One of the women screamed and several of the children cried. Angela shuffled toward what she hoped was the table. After sticking her fingers in several sandwiches she located the box of candles. To her surprise she even found a lighter. She grabbed a handful of candles, lit one, and started to hand out and light the others. A soft glow filled the room. It reminded her of childhood Christmas Eves when she and Tony went to church and sang carols. Those were wonderful times. What had happened to change them?

A little girl was huddled alone in a dark corner with her head pressed between her knees. Angela handed her a candle and asked which of the women was her mother.

"I don't have a mother," sobbed the girl. "My mother and father were killed in Iraq and now I live with my uncle but he's a policeman and he's at work and I'm all alone."

The girl was shaking uncontrollably so Angela took her in her arms, rocked her back and forth, and sang a lullaby she didn't know she knew. "Hush little baby, don't you cry . . ."

Angela and Carl had never had children. According to him, they were expensive, dirty, and totally unnecessary. He said goats and chickens were easier to care for than children. If any of the animals misbehaved you simply shut them up in a cage or slaughtered them. Problem solved. If they had had a daughter, would she have looked like this girl?

The wind had been growing stronger but it suddenly stopped and the air grew thick. The only sound was the eerie wail of car alarms. Everyone looked toward the Rabbi.

"We're in the eye of the storm," he whispered. "Everyone stay where you are."

Angela cuddled the girl closer in her arms.

"Are we going to die?" asked the girl.

"No, sweetheart," replied Angela. "Not if I can help it."

A few minutes later a thunderous blast ripped through the silence and a hole appeared in the ceiling. The wind shrieked and moaned. It sounded like a freight train barreling through the building. The hole grew larger, and rain started pouring in.

Angela's heart was pounding and she couldn't catch her breath. She wanted to run but she knew she had to protect the child. She tried placing her body over the girl's but the child was still getting wet. As if out of nowhere, Tony and Fran appeared at her side and together the three of them wrapped their bodies around the girl.

The building began to shake. Trees smashed into the walls, windows crashed, beams fell, transformers exploded, and everything in the path of the savage beast was shredded and turned into deadly missiles. Angela began to think the little girl was right and that she and everyone in that room were going to die. She had lived a long life, but the girl was so young. It was too soon for God to take this child home. There were so many things for her to learn, so many places for her to go, so many people for her to meet.

One of the men began singing. Soon the others joined him. Even though Angela didn't understand the words, she sensed their meaning. She didn't want to cry because she knew it would frighten the little girl but she couldn't hold back her tears.

The girl reached up and touched Angela's face. "Don't cry, lady. God will watch over us."

Angela hugged the girl tighter and asked, "Can you teach us the words to that song?"

"Hash-ki-vey-nu Ado-nai E-lo-hey . . ." The girl sang slowly while Angela, Fran, and Tony listened. Her voice was soft, quiet, almost angelic.

"What does that mean?" asked Fran.

"Let there be love and understanding. May peace and friendship be our shelter," replied the girl. "God loves His people. He will take care of us."

All her life, Angela thought people tried to use her for their own selfish reasons but the truth was they were only trying to help her because they cared about her. True, the kid back in Indiana used her to get ahead at work and Carl tried to take advantage of her so he could buy another farm, but not everyone was like them. Tony had talked her into moving to Florida because he was trying to help her. And Katherine, crazy as she was, was only concerned with having fun. What was wrong with that?

Even down in this basement, strangers offered what little they had and didn't ask for anything in return. Everyone took care of everyone else — no strings attached. What they couldn't handle, they left to God and they trusted that He would be there for them. Was this the reason she had come to

Florida? Was this what she needed to see?

After what seemed like hours, it became quiet again. The people stopped singing and looked around. Tony and Fran moved away from the girl but Angela stayed where she was.

"Is it over?" she whispered.

"Yes, I think so," replied the rabbi as he brushed dust from his black vest.

Tony and Fran stood up and began checking to make sure everyone was all right. A couple of children cried, but no one complained of being hurt.

It was still raining but the sun was shining through the hole in the ceiling. Angela craned her neck, looked up at the sky, and saw a rainbow. It was a good sign.

A siren pierced the air and came to a stop outside the synagogue. Heavy footsteps pounded the stairs and then the basement door was thrown open.

"Is everyone okay?" It was the state trooper who stopped Tony on the interstate.

The little girl broke loose from Angela's grip and ran toward him. "Uncle Aaron, Uncle Aaron. That lady over there sang to me and those other people kept me dry." She pointed toward Angela, Fran, and Tony.

"Well, looks like I chose the right guy to pull over," the trooper laughed. "Now what

say I get all you nice people out of here?"
He lifted the girl into his arms and led the
way out of the basement.

When the group reached the upper floor,
they discovered that most of the roof and
three of the walls were gone. It looked like
everything in the synagogue had been
destroyed. Everything except the Eternal
Lamp.

20
THE AFTERMATH

Tony heaved a sigh of relief. "Looks like we got lucky."

"Lucky?" Angela couldn't believe her ears. All around the trailer park, all she saw were broken windows, mutilated palm trees, and overturned golf carts. The doctor's and Tony's trailers had survived with little more than loose shingles but several others were totally roofless.

"Yeah, the hurricane turned away just before it hit land and all we got was the tail end."

"If that was the tail end, I'm glad I didn't see its face."

Angela walked toward the front of her trailer and picked up the remains of a hanging planter. "Well, this one's a goner." She held the planter up for Tony to see. One lonely pansy stuck its head up proudly.

"I wouldn't worry," mumbled Tony. "All the stores will be selling new ones in a couple of days." He was already taking the plywood off Angela's doors and windows. "How about giving me a hand? The sooner we get done here the sooner I can go home and jump into the shower. That shelter was a little short on amenities if you know what I mean."

"True. But they were nice people weren't they?" She grabbed a hammer and started yanking at screws.

"I guess." Tony hung his head and became unusually silent.

"Are you all right?" Angela was afraid something was wrong with her brother. Driving through the storm and trying to find a place to get out of it had been stressful. Maybe his heart was acting up again.

"I'm okay. It's just that I feel bad about what I put you through."

"What? The storm wasn't your fault, was it?" Angela shook her head in confusion.

"No. But Carl was."

"Oh. That. Well, you couldn't have stopped him from leaving."

"No, but I could have stopped him from coming."

"What do you mean?" Angela kept right on working.

"When Carl found out you left Indiana, he called me to see if I knew where you were. He said he still loved you and wanted to get back with you so I told him you were here and suggested he come down and talk to you."

"You already told me all that, Tony. The thing I never understood was why you thought I would even want to see him." She wedged her hammer under a sheet of plywood and lifted. Several nails popped out.

"You seemed so fragile and unsure of yourself. I was afraid that if anything happened to me, you'd fall apart."

"Hey . . . I've just been through a major hurricane. Do I look like I'm falling apart?" Angela felt strangely exhilarated. She had lived through her worst nightmare and survived. She had a new lease on life and she wanted to enjoy every minute of it.

"That's just it. I underestimated you."

"Oh, don't be so hard on yourself, Tony." She yanked at a stubborn nail.

"Let me get this off my chest, will ya?" He seemed determined to tell her everything.

"Sorry. Go ahead." Angela laid down her hammer and focused on her brother.

"When we were kids, Mom and Dad weren't around much so I sort of ended up taking over for them. I walked you to school, helped you with your homework, I even taught you how to ride a bike."

"Yeah. I remember. About the only thing you didn't do was take part in my dolly tea parties."

Tony didn't smile. "I didn't mind at first but when you got older and started dating, I felt like you turned your back on me."

"You're kidding." Angela would have laughed if Tony hadn't looked so serious.

"No, I'm not. I was your one and only brother. You were supposed to look up to me."

"That's ridiculous, Tony."

"Maybe, but I always thought you needed someone to take care of you and until Carl came along I was that person."

Angela stared at her brother wondering how far he was going to take this.

"When you and Carl got married, I figured I was finally off the hook but when your marriage fell apart and you started calling me for advice, I was right back where I started."

Angela knew her brother had always given advice without having to be asked but she thought better than to argue the point. Tony was hurting and needed to clear his conscience. "Why didn't you say something sooner?" she asked.

"Like I said . . . I'm your big brother and

I'm supposed to be strong."

"You always have been, Tony, and I love you for it. I'll admit growing up was tough and there were plenty of times I needed your help but now I'm an adult and I can stand on my own two feet."

"I know. You proved that today when you tried to protect that little girl. You were getting drenched by the rain and your only thought was about her. That's when I realized that if it wasn't for me, you would never have been in that spot. I was the one who talked you into moving to Florida and I was the one who called Carl. I felt like I had to protect you but when Fran and I tried to help, I saw you already had everything under control. You were all grown up and you didn't need me anymore. Have I lost you, Angela?"

Angela wrapped her arms around her brother. "There's no way you'll ever lose me, Tony. Others may come and go but brothers and sisters are forever." She gave him a big kiss then smiled and pushed him away. "Now go home and take that shower. You're smelling my place up."

Tony started walking away but stopped in his tracks, turned around, and yelled, "I love you, little sister."

"I love you back, big brother," she whispered.

Angela went back to work removing the plywood. Just as she got to the last sheet she heard a familiar sound. It was Gizmo barking at the top of his lungs and dragging Katherine behind him.

"Come and get this dog before he yanks my arm off," screamed Katherine.

Angela dropped the hammer and went running to the dog. Getting down on her knees, she hugged and kissed him while he wiggled from ears to tail.

"Gizmo," she sobbed. "I thought I'd lost you. Where were you? Are you all right?" With tears streaming down her cheeks, she ran her hands over the dog's body to make sure nothing was broken.

"Hey — don't I get a hello?" Katherine tried to act offended but her toothy grin gave her away.

Angela jumped to her feet and hugged her redheaded friend. "Oh, Katherine. You're so wonderful. How can I ever thank you? Where did you find Gizmo?"

"Mongo spotted him running loose near the dog walking area. He grabbed him and tried to take him home but your trailer was boarded up and no one was inside so he brought him back to our place. I tried calling you a couple of times but then the phones went out so I thought I'd just take a walk and see if you were home. And guess what? You are."

"Yes. We just got back a little while ago."

"Where'd you go?"

"Well, Tony was trying to drive us up north someplace but the roads were all backed up so he turned around and then we got stopped by a state trooper and . . . Hey? Want a cup of coffee or something?"

"Thought you'd never ask."

Katherine and Angela followed as Gizmo raced into the trailer. After checking behind every door and around every corner, the dog headed for his favorite sleeping spot, circled twice, laid down, sighed, and went to sleep. There was no question. He was glad to be home.

"Well, I'll be," laughed Katherine. "Doesn't anything faze that dog?"

"Just rainstorms and high winds," replied Angela. "That's probably why he ran." She filled the coffeepot with water and flipped the on-switch. Nothing happened.

"Dah," snickered Katherine. "I forgot to tell you. The power is off, too."

"How's orange juice?"

"Fresh?" asked Katherine.

"We're still in Florida, right?"

Angela grabbed a couple of oranges, squeezed them into two glasses, added some half-melted ice cubes, and motioned toward the front door. "Let's go outside and enjoy the sunshine." After being cooped up for hours in the synagogue basement, she wanted to spend as much time outdoors as possible.

"So, come on girl, tell me what happened. Where'd you guys end up?"

Almost as glad to be home as her dog, Angela kicked her shoes off and leaned back in her chair. "Well, like I said, Tony got pulled over when he tried to turn around and the trooper led us to a synagogue."

"You mean Jewish. Like in Carl?"

"Ironic, isn't it? Carl ran off and left me and a bunch of Jewish people saved me."

"Carl ran off?" Katherine's eyes bulged.

"That's a whole other story. The big thing was the way everyone at that synagogue treated us. They gave us food and shelter and they didn't act like we were strangers. The rabbi told stories, we prayed together, we even sang songs. It was like we were all family."

"So, what? Now you're gonna turn Jewish?"

"No. It's just that while I was in that basement, I realized I've spent my whole life looking for something that was always right in front of me. All I had to do was open my eyes."

"What are you talking about, Angela? Did you get hit on the head or something?"

"No, I did not. But once I looked around, I realized I had always been surrounded by people who cared about me. My parents, Tony, all my friends while I was growing up, even you and Mongo."

"Gee, thanks," grumbled Katherine.

"Even down in that dark basement, in the middle of a hurricane, I wasn't alone. Call me silly but I even felt like there was some sort of strange presence in that room. I don't know if it was love or what, but whatever it was, I knew that it was what I needed — what I had always needed. It was a whole new feeling for me and for the first time in my life I felt safe. And you know what? It made me want to live."

"Well, hallelujah. There's hope for you yet."

"What do you mean?" asked Angela.

"When we first met, it looked like you'd been through a lot and were a little bummed out on life. You were so pitiful, I thought if you had a little excitement in your life, you'd enjoy it more. That's why I dragged you down to Key West and tried to get you interested in the Foxy Ladies."

"You mean there was a method to your madness?"

"Of course."

"And all this time I thought you were just using me to help pick up men."

"Well, that. But I was also trying to get you out of that protective shell you built around yourself."

"What shell?"

"Don't act dumb, Angela. You know what I'm talking about."

"Yeah, I do know. It's just that sometimes it's easier to hide than to stand all alone out in the open."

"But you're not all alone."

"And I never was. There was always someone around to help me."

"Ya think?"

"Yeah, I think. But enough about me. What about you and Mongo? Why didn't you evacuate?"

"Mongo was worried about his rabbits."

"His rabbits?"

"Oh, that's right, you don't know. Steve and Monica bought an old church in West Virginia. It's so far back in the hollows that some of the people who live there haven't been to church in years. Steve says he'll hold services in the church and Monica will raise a garden and sell vegetables."

"Monica's gonna grow a garden?"

"Like they say, 'Seeing is believing.' Anyway, when Mongo heard about the farm he told Monica she should breed rabbits. Something about there being big money in rabbit fur. Monica said 'No thanks' but Mongo decided to raise some little bunnies and give them to her as a sort of house warming gift."

"How thoughtful," laughed Angela. "So did the rabbits survive?"

"No. They drowned." Katherine bit her tongue to keep from laughing.

"Shame on you, Katherine."

"I know. I'm bad. Anyway, Mongo says he'll try again."

"Good for him. When are Steve and Monica leaving?"

"Probably by the end of summer. Mongo should have a whole herd by then."

"I don't think rabbits come in herds," laughed Angela.

"Whatever." Katherine finished her orange juice in one gulp.

"So what about the rest of the park? Did everyone make it through okay?"

Katherine raised her eyebrows. "You mean like Gilberto?"

"Him . . . and everyone else." Angela tried

to act nonchalant.

"The Smiths over on Peacock lost their shed and the Websters had several smashed windows. I haven't seen Gil yet but I'm sure he's okay. He was over at Mrs. Snodgrass' place."

"I saw him with her at Home Depot. Can you believe? She was buying a plant."

"That poor woman. She hasn't been well since her son died."

"He died? When?"

"Oh, several years ago. Some kind of boating accident. They never found his body."

Angela looked confused. "But she always talks about her son taking her shopping and doing things for her."

"When her son died, she sort of lost it. She started talking about aliens and spaceships and some of the people in her park suggested having her committed. When Gil found out, he took it upon himself to take care of her. He buys her groceries, he pays her bills, and he even takes her to church. I guess she thinks he's her son."

"That's so sad." Angela absentmindedly sipped her juice.

"Yes, but Gil doesn't seem to mind. He's really a great guy. Aside from taking care of Mrs. Snodgrass, he teaches English as a second language, serves lunch twice a week at the homeless shelter, and as you no doubt remember, volunteers at the Turtle Hospital down in Marathon. If I didn't already have a boyfriend, I'd set my cap for that one."

"I didn't know he did all those things. I guess that explains why he's gone so much of the time. Tony always said it was because he was nothing but an aging lothario."

"Aging yes, lothario no. Sure, he was married a couple of times but both his wives died from cancer." Katherine had that smug "I know everything, just ask me" look on her face.

"Cancer? He told me his wives left him." Why hadn't he told her the truth?

"Well, in a sense, I guess they did."

All at once, everything became crystal clear. The night they met, Angela had carried on about all her problems — being divorced, having to make it on her own, being passed over for a promotion, and having to drive all the way to Florida alone. How could she have been so insensitive? If Gil had told her about losing his wives to cancer, she might have felt sorry for him. She had so many problems of her own he obviously didn't want to burden her with his. Just like Tony, the Rabbi, and everyone else in her life, Gil really cared about her. Katherine was right. Gilberto Fontero was a great guy but she had run him off.

"Oh, Katherine. How could I have been so wrong? I thought Gil was trying to come between me and Carl but he was only trying to protect me. He knew Carl was trying to take advantage of me and he didn't want me to get hurt again. Then he and Carl got into that awful fight and I told him to stay out of my life. I should have known better than to trust Carl, but no, I jumped right in and look what happened. I think I really messed up this time. What am I going to do?"

Katherine stood up and placed her hand on Angela's shoulder. "Well, for starters, try turning around."

Angela turned. There on the sidewalk stood a svelte-looking gentleman wearing an azure blue shirt (open to the third button) with white trousers that had sharp creases but no wrinkles. In his hands was an overflowing platter of antipasto.

"*Ciao.* My name is Gilberto Fontero and I would like to welcome you to Egret Cove."

Angela smiled.

She was truly home.

READERS' GUIDE

1. Have you ever lived in a trailer park? Did you enjoy it?

2. Do you like Italian food? What about Italian men?

3. Would you ever consider getting a tattoo? What and where might it be?

4. How do you feel about self-defense classes? Do you think they're necessary?

5. Have you ever been on a cruise? To where?

6. Have you ever been in a hurricane? Did it frighten you?

7. How does Angela really feel about her brother?

8. Why was Angela so attached to her dog?

9. Is it appropriate for women of a "certain age" to get tattoos?

10. Do you think there are unwritten laws older women should live by?

11. Was Angela's ex trying to take advantage of her?

12. Do you think Angela should get married again?

ABOUT THE AUTHOR

Margaret Nava is the author of two southwestern U.S. travel guides, *Along The High Road* and *Remembering.* Her love for visiting new places led her to write her first novel, *Egret Cove,* about the adventures of Angela Dunn and her dog, Gizmo. Margaret is at work on more novels about Angela and Gizmo's travels. You can learn more about Angela and her friends at www.angeladunn.homestead.com or E-mail her at angeladunn08@aol.com.

We hope you have enjoyed this Large Print book. Other Thorndike, Wheeler, Kennebec, and Chivers Press Large Print books are available at your library or directly from the publishers.

For information about current and upcoming titles, please call or write, without obligation, to:

Publisher
Thorndike Press
295 Kennedy Memorial Drive
Waterville, ME 04901
Tel. (800) 223-1244

or visit our Web site at:

http://gale.cengage.com/thorndike

OR

Chivers Large Print
published by BBC Audiobooks Ltd
St James House, The Square
Lower Bristol Road
Bath BA2 3SB
England
Tel. +44(0) 800 136919
email: bbcaudiobooks@bbc.co.uk
www.bbcaudiobooks.co.uk

All our Large Print titles are designed for easy reading, and all our books are made to last.